SNAKEHAND

SNAKEHAND

THE SIDEWINDERS BOOK 1

Chuck Dixon
&
John Neal

CASTALIA HOUSE

Snakehand (The Sidewinders, Book 1)
Chuck Dixon and John Neal

Published by Castalia House
Switzerland

ISBN: 978-952-7303-33-7

Contents

1

The train of wagons trundled along a switchback that rounded the base of the butte. Big sturdy freight wagons weighed down beneath loads belted tight under tarps. Twelve mule teams. Heavy cargo. A dun-colored cloud of dust rose behind them to form a column high into the yellow sky.

"What they hauling?" young Joe asked of Ben Temple lying prone beside him on a rock shelf high above the trail. Ben had a long brass telescope trained on the silent parade below. A flap of hide was bound with twine to the front of the scope to shade the glass. No one below would see any telltale flash off the lens.

"Don't know. A lot of something. And a lot of anything is worth having," Ben said, open eye screwed to the lens.

Joe Wiley lay watching Ben study the scene below. Ben was a big, broad-shouldered man with a thick black beard and hair to his collar. The telescope looked small, like a toy, in his hands. His face was burnt as dark as a native, dark as walnut from a life in the sun and wind. His light gray eyes were all the more noticeable in that dusky countenance.

Joe shifted, anxious for a look through the glass. He was as restless and antsy as Ben was composed and measured. He was a decade, or more, younger than the other man. No way to tell how many years he had, really. He was nearly a man and longed to be seen as such by the other men in the outfit. Ben Temple most of all. Joe was red as a

Comanche himself with the contrast of a shock of sun-bleached hair that hung to his shoulders. His body was rangy and slim. There was speed and power there and he ached to move, to make something happen. But Ben lay still, pondering what he saw below them, and Joe was obliged to do the same.

At last, Ben handed the scope to Joe.

Joe found the wagons after a dizzying search down the rock wall through the lens. A driver, hands filled with the straps of a team of twelve, filled his vision. Beside the driver sat a man with a big double-barrel coach gun across his knees.

"See the ruts they're leaving. Deep. That's a shitload of goods in those wagons," Ben said.

Joe swung the glass to see the furrows in the clay left by the steel-rimmed wheels.

"And those pistoleros. They're not there to watch over hay wagons," Ben said.

Joe moved his view around to take in the outriders that flanked the column of wagons. Each rider was festooned with pistols on their hips and more mounted on their saddles. Each rode with a rifle or shotgun laid ready against the pommel. Their heads moved as though on swivels, watching the land all about for an ambush or sign. Before the head of the column rode a phalanx of armed men with more spread out riding behind.

"Professionals through and through," Ben said.

"You thought of how we might take them?" Joe said, eyes still trained below.

"We're not jumping them on while they're in column. That's for damned sure. Like taking on a company of dragoons."

"So when?"

"When the prevailing conditions are properly aligned to favor us rather than them," Ben said, lying on his back now, head resting on his arms, booted feet crossed. Ben Temple was book learned and he often spoke using words that young Joe took some time to decipher.

"We follow them?" Joe said, taking his eyes from the lens.

"That's what we're going to do, boy," Ben said and closed his eyes, making no move to rise.

Joe turned the scope back on the train of wagons. It rounded the curved wall of the butte, heading west. He watched until the last wagon was gone. The drag riders trotted through the trailing veil of dust and were soon out of sight on the other side of the rock face.

"They're gone away around the butte, following the dry wash," Joe said and rose to a crouch. He pressed the telescope closed and placed it in Ben's open hand.

"That means they'll be turning north, should they continue on that course. We'll give them some time and follow along through the pines," Ben said, placing the scope in a tooled leather case. He sat up and set his dusty sombrero atop his head, pressing it down on his hair and securing the chin strap. Joe put on his own broad-brimmed hat and together they left the edge of the escarpment, rifles in hand, taking care to remain low so as not to skyline themselves to anyone watching the rim rock.

The others were waiting in a tree-shaded gully below. A half hundred men and half again as many mounts. They were coarse men, wild men. They resembled a pack of wolves more than a gang of outlaws. More a gang of mongrels. There were white men, Mexicans, Kiowa and Neches, and mixes of all or some of those breeds. There were even a few blacks, runaways from the fields around Austin. Any man who could ride, shoot and live rough was welcome. Any man who couldn't cut it was left behind.

Indian ponies snuffled and huffed as the men stirred. They sensed the tension in the men and joined them in their mood of hushed anticipation.

"What is it, Temple? What did you see?" Muñoz called, stepping from the shadows of a pine.

Muñoz claimed to have Castilian blood from Old Spain. To Joe he looked like any other Mex peon—only crossed with a scorpion. He wore filthy white peon sackcloth cinched tight with a frayed gun belt from which a long-barreled Colt hung over his crotch. On his feet were tooled leather riding boots with silver spurs. He claimed he took them from the feet of the don that owned the rancho where Muñoz was once a serf.

"A fat train of teamster wagons moving west and north along the creek bed trail. Heading up to the territories is what I reckon," Ben said, walking to his own mount, a pinto mare with black mane and tail.

"How fat?" This from Ryderdale, a Texican who still wore the jacket of the American army company he'd deserted a year earlier.

"Ten wagons. Twelve dray mules each. Loaded down with goods," Ben said, checking the saddle cinch. Sliding his Enfield rifle back into its scabbard. Patting the pony's neck.

"*Hay mujeres*?" Muñoz called out.

"No women, you rutting buck," Ben said with a smile. The Mexican cursed a streak in gutter Spanish. Some of the men laughed.

"And riders. Men with guns," Joe piped up. Ben shot him a look. Joe lowered his eyes to the pine needles beneath his moccasins.

"Army riders?" Muñoz said. The men in the gloom of the trees muttered to one another.

"Hired men. Pistoleros. I counted twenty. With the drivers and wagon guards that makes forty," Ben said, eyeing the men gathering around him.

"You have an idea of how to take them or do we let them ride on?" Ryderdale said.

"The hell we let them ride on!" Muñoz barked. Some of the others, Mexes mostly, nodded agreement.

"We dog them. They have to camp somewhere come dark. If the ground is right, we take those goods off their hands," Ben said, and mounted his pinto.

Muñoz let out a yip that was echoed among the other Mexes and bucks.

Young Joe was on the back of his roan and followed close behind Ben Temple as they trotted beneath the trees, turning north to where the high ground sloped down to meet the valley floor. Ben took lead and set the pace for the rest. They rode at a walk, allowing the horses to pick their way over the stubble and rocks. Given their head, the men would have raced after the wagons, eager to be at the loads they held in their beds. Only that would have risked the wrath of their chief and they knew the outcome of doing that. Ben Temple was not a man to cross. Not even once.

Joe had seen the carcasses of many men who either defied, challenged or disobeyed Ben Temple's will. The back trail as far as the Brazos was littered with men who had done so. They lay unmourned where they fell, stripped of their valuables and left for the coyotes and buzzards. His law was their only law, and that law was backed by his gun and the guns of Muñoz and Ryderdale, his lieutenants.

So, they moved together down the wooded defile, not like the pack of mongrel dogs they were but more like a pride of *tigres* stalking their prey, silent and sure in the midday gloom of the forest.

2

Young Joe Wiley's first memories were of fights. He sometimes thought he was born fighting.

He was one of a rabble of bastards living in the camps that came and went outside Bent's Fort. They lived like dogs on the scraps and leavings of traders, trappers, hunters, Indians and soldiers. Sometimes they even fought with the stray dogs for a sliver of meat or a buffalo joint. Mostly they fought each other and often to the amusement of the men who made rendezvous around the collection of adobe buildings. They lived in lean-tos, tents and wickiups.

Joe was remarkable for being purebred white. Most of the other unwanted children were from one of the tribes or of mixed blood. They were left behind by squaws who either died or abandoned them to live or die. They were the unwanted product of laying with soldiers or trappers in exchange for a strip of cloth, a length of copper wire or a drink of company rum. Girls died soonest. Only the toughest of the boys made it to adulthood.

And Joe was a tough one, an untamed cub who could snatch a greasy handful of meat and be away before the others could catch him. Or, failing to escape with his prize, would attack with teeth, fists and feet until he was either beaten down or left in peace to chew his slice of gristly steak.

It was his feral nature and fearless stripe that made Ben Temple take notice of him. That and Joe's mane of white, blond hair atop the filthy, half-naked hide of the bestial child. At the time Ben was making his living as a buffalo hunter under contract to the army. He was at Bent's Fort often on his rounds, returning to the post with ox carts loaded down with trimmed meat to be salted and tanned hides to be traded.

Temple and his crew of hunters and skinners would stay a week or more in camp near the fort. They'd drink and smoke and rut with squaws before setting out north or south or west to follow the herds. They'd fight as well. With other trappers and hunters or soldiers or each other. Men died by the campfires, shot down or brained or gutted over the remains of a bottle or the attentions of a whore. Sometimes they died for no reason that anyone could recall. The only thing that anyone could remember was whether it was a good fight or a bad fight. Did the man who lost die well or die poorly was the only consideration. More than skill or toughness, the men who looked on wished most dearly that the man who fell to the fists, blade or ball not die whimpering and so bring shame to them all for having seen it happen.

So, it was a fight that first made Ben Temple pay closer mind to the towheaded bastard he'd seen running around the camps on previous visits.

One night, Joe had leapt for a rib of bison discarded by a drunken hunter. It was a long bone with a clump of stringy meat still clinging to one end. He jumped, hands clawing, only to take the sole of a foot in the face that set him rolling. A taller, older boy picked up the scrap and walked from the shared cook fire. It was an Indian named Stork for his height. He was two heads taller than Joe and a few years older. Joe charged him anyway. The pair tumbled to the ground together with feet and fists flying. They rolled as one toward the fire. Hooting and calling, the men seated in a ring rose to make way for them.

Ben Temple watched the boys fight over the rib even though it had already vanished from where it was dropped in the dirt; taken by another boy who raced away into the dark hugging the prize to his chest.

The men around the fire shouted and laughed as the boys grunted and squealed, locked in combat. Ben shouldered through the mass for a closer look. The smaller boy drove a knee into the other's groin and landed his full weight on it while, at the same time, hooking a thumb in the other's boy's mouth and pulling hard at a corner. Stork pawed for young Joe's eyes, squealing at the pain lancing up from his crushed testicles. He rocked back and forth, jerking to escape the terrible pressure but the smaller boy rode him with a tenacious fury. Joe snapped at the fingers of the reaching hands, taking a pinkie between his teeth and biting down hard. With a vicious yank on the soft flesh of Stork's cheek, young Joe ripped a gash in the corner of his mouth. A geyser of blood sprayed up painting Joe crimson. Stork let out a gurgling scream and pounded the ground with the flat of his hand until the boy stood up, releasing him.

A roar rose from about the fire, an animal exultation at the bloody spectacle from a hundred throats. Joe got pats on the back and men ruffled his hair like a prized fighting dog. They fed him with strips of roasted meat and wild potatoes and corn mush. They pressed him to sip from their bottles until Ben Temple stepped in to pull the boy away.

"You'll kill him with that liquor, you idiots," Ben growled. And, drunk as they were, they took Ben's rebuke in high spirits.

"What's your name, boy?" Ben said.

Young Joe remained mum, mouth chewing the fine steak he'd been given. Face smeared with mush and grease.

Ben spoke to the others. "Does he have a name? Anyone hear know a name for him?"

"I mostly hear him called Wily Joe. 'Cause he's the slickest of all these little shits." This from a pie-eyed soldier, speaking with a lazy Tennessee drawl.

"Joe Wiley. Suits you," Ben said, a thumb under the boy's chin to study his face.

And they were together, man and boy, from that night forward.

3

The teamster camp lay under a star-filled sky spread about the nimbus glow of a quarter moon. The laden wagons were all secured. The horses and mules all seen to; gathered in a remuda of ropes strung in a square to wagons serving as posts at each corner. A guttering cook fire threw dancing shadows over the sleeping men. A half dozen guards were awake. Some smoked in the shadows near the wagons. Other stood post on the rocky ground beyond the fire.

Out in the wild dark, Ben Temple kept his wolves at bay. A slow-moving bank of clouds crossed the sliver of moon, throwing the camp into deeper gloom. Temple gave a low whistle in imitation of a woodcock. The men about him moved low toward the slumbering camp.

Young Joe Wiley was struck at how quiet it all was. No sound save the flapping of an unsecured piece of canvas in the breeze. And the crack and pop of the cook fire. The first targets were the men standing watch. They never stood a chance. Muñoz emerged from the shadows in the gorse brush to garrote one to the left of Joe. Ben dropped from a shelf of rock to cut the throat of another.

All of his life Joe had been fighting for scraps of food and for his very survival. He never took joy from hurting another man or even killing one. It wasn't a choice one had the freedom to make in this hard land. And, like any task he put his mind to, he became expert at it. Time and nature had provided him with a lean muscular form that powered him with more speed and strength than the wolf cub

Ben Temple had taken away from Bent's Fort behind the cantle of his saddle all those years before. Joe was anxious to prove himself to the other men and to Ben Temple especially. He longed to be one of Ben's lieutenants. Not just an eager kid tagging along Ben's back trail. He was confident that he could better serve Ben than the two he had now, particularly Muñoz.

Unseen in the poor light, the few of the renegade Indians among them were dispatching their chosen targets.

Joe quietly and efficiently murdered the lookout he'd chosen to attack. A hand clapped over the man's mouth. The point of a spade-shaped blade driven into the base of the man's skull. A punch upward through bone and gristle. A twist of the point in the soft meat of the brain. He glanced down at the now dead man and then stepped over him. He looked to Ben, seeking his approval and the next silent command. Ben nodded and gave the signal for the others to close in.

Somewhere in the unfamiliar dark one of the raiders tripped over a rope line sending a water bucket and some pans crashing. Shapes about the fire moved, jerking to life. The teamsters and pistoleros emerged from their bedding, some clad in their long drawers and some riders in short britches. They came awake with blades and firearms in their fists. The sleeping camp roused to chaos. It was a close quarters gunfight, the two sides clashed in a struggle for their lives. The men of the camp couldn't be certain from which direction the danger came and so lit the night with fire in all directions. The thunder was returned by the attackers. A drifting pall of smoke from the combined discharges fell over the circle of wagons. The raiders rushed howling from the sulfurous cloud like the host of Satan.

Diego, a short, stout, long term member of Temple's raiders, took a bullet to his heart and fell dead at Joe's feet. A spray of black blood from his mouth as he kicked out his last. Another of the raiders was lifted clean off the ground by a load of shot. The force was enough to send one of the man's boots flying from his foot. Other men cursed in fury or mewled in terror. Bodies fell to the ground as hot lead filled the air while the desperate men on both sides attempted to kill the other. The smell of gun smoke and blood was pungent, as was the piss of those who lay dead. The fight seemed like an eternity in the moment but actually was a flash of motion and fury, men shooting, knifing, clawing and killing each other in the wild confusion.

Joe moved low with a pair of Colts in his fists and the bloody blade of his dagger pressed between his lips. He looked around and took aim at a bawling shadow moving in the stinking mist. The man fell with a shriek. Flashes lit the night near where the man fell. Joe heard the rushing wind of a lead ball sail close by his head. Rather than cower, he stood full height and let off a string of shots from both pistols held at arm's length. He ran for the cover of a wagon, leaping over bodies as he moved. The wicket and strike of hot rounds followed close behind.

The gunfire was more deliberate now as the two opposing sides took the measure of one another. This was high tide. This was where the fight was won or lost. In the dark and the smoke and sheer madness of it all, Joe could not sense in whose favor the tide was turning. For all he knew half of his company was down or dead or run off. It might only be him and a couple others left, waiting for the teamsters and their hired guns to come out and shoot them down like rabid dogs.

It was then Joe spied Ben charging across the camp, black with blood, his long-barreled Remington sending out a gout of flame. Joe moved closer to Ben dodging from cover to cover, what meager cover there was. As he ran, he saw a rail thin pistolero slithering from beneath a wagon tongue that lay angled to the ground. The man reminded him of a snake. Joe couldn't help but admire the other man's gun and rig as the pistolero rose to a knee and fired. Two slugs knocked down one of the raiders, a half-breed Mex Irishman named Ramon O'Hara, a man quick with a joke and well-liked by the others.

Joe shot the slim gunman twice as he ran to close the gap between them. The first ball spun the man to the side. The second struck the man in the face, sending a saucer sized section of skull flying from the back of the pistolero's head. Joe moved past him. He did not begrudge the man for killing his friend. This was a fight to the death. But he would miss O'Hara at the next campfire to be sure, his stories and his laughter. That made killing the man all that much easier.

The noise rose as the fury of the battle swelled to echo off the rocks with the blast of guns and the yells of men. War whoops yipped from a few of the Indians. Joe caught sight of Ben, Muñoz with him. Both men walked with deliberation toward the last defenders holed up beneath a wagon. They fired as they walked, ignoring gouts of dust kicked up about them. A teamster rose from under the wagon's belly with a long rifle to his shoulder. Muñoz brought him down with a shot to the throat; the man dropped gurgling and spewing.

Joe trotted forward, only one Colt with any charges left in it. He raised this with the front tang toward the source of gunfire coming from around the last wagon. He saw a shape grow from the peak of the hummock of the cargo load atop the wagon. The clouds moved past the sliver moon in time to reveal it was a man standing in the sylvan glow, feet braced atop the load. A big-gutted teamster with a ten-gauge coach gun aimed square down at Ben Temple.

"It's over for you. You murdering son of a whore!" the man shouted.

"Ben! Behind you!" Joe Wiley shouted.

Ben turned around, whip fast to raise a pistol at the man looming above him.

And the hammer fell with a dull click on a spent chamber.

4

Joe dropped his spent Colt to free his hand to fan the hammer of the one remaining.

His first wild shot round took the fat teamster in the thigh, causing the man to stumble back on his uncertain perch. The coach gun in the man's fists discharged, sending shot and flame into the sky. The second ball went high into the man's chest and spilled him backwards off the top of the wagon and out of sight.

Ben whirled to where Joe stood, smoking Colt in his hand, eyes wide and feral. Ben's eyes narrowed and he tilted his head in a swift appraisal. Joe's grin grew wider around the dagger blade still clenched in his teeth.

A coyote whoop sounded high over the camp. A big Tonkawa buck charged into the guttering firelight leading a phalanx of raiders on horseback. Wolf, the Tonkawa, raised a rifle over his head and shrieked like a mad man. The teamsters and pistoleros broke off their fire and ran from cover into the surrounding dark with only a few parting snap shots. The mounted men pursued the scattering defenders.

Ben and Muñoz raced after them on foot with Joe behind the charge. Joe tossed his remaining Colt aside. He snatched up a long-barreled revolver from the hand of a man sitting against a wagon wheel with half his head gone. He ran to catch up.

From the shadows rose the shouts of men exulting in victory along with the screams of men dying.

Joe caught up with Ben. The older man was crouching, head down. A few of the other raiders, white men and Mexicans, stood afoot gazing into the impenetrable blackness of the night. Laughter echoed off the rocks. Beneath it the mewling of pleading men gibbering for their lives. They'd soon be begging to die.

"Muñoz is with them," Ben said as Joe dropped to one knee by him. "Damned dago's as bloodthirsty as those savages."

Joe said nothing. Ben was speaking for only him to hear.

"A more Christian fella would go out there and put a bullet in every one of those bastards," Ben said, "Only I'm so damned tired."

Joe wasn't sure if Ben was speaking of the tortured or the torturers. Ben turned and fixed Joe with a squint.

"I must have known this night was coming somehow. Back then, at Bent's Fort. Must have seen you were my guardian angel." The corner of Ben's mouth turned up in a smile.

"I'm your guardian angel?" Joe said.

"Well it's for sure heaven hasn't assigned a poor damned soul like me any special favors," Ben said. "Had to get myself one."

They returned to the wagon camp, leaving the animal squeals behind them. The looting of the wagons and corpses had already begun.

Men were tearing aside the canvas covers from the wagons and rooting through the loads. They tossed fat bundles to the ground. The bundles were wrapped in oil skins and tied with cords. A few were cut open to reveal stacks of folded blankets inside. Others held bolts of woolen cloth. Wooden crates were being lifted down from another wagon with greater care. Ryderdale was standing by the smoky fire, a bottle in his hand.

"Real Kentucky whiskey, Temple. Cases of it packed in straw," Ryderdale roared. The Texican tipped the bottle back to take a mouthful that he spat in a stream into the fire. Flames exploded, sending a swirling column of embers high into the air.

"How many did we lose?" Ben said.

"I seed Briggs fall with a bellyful of buck. Couple others. That fella from Galveston said he was a sailor. And that Mex with the buck teeth," Ryderdale said.

"Diego," Joe said.

"That's the one," Ryderdale said and took another long swallow.

Ben stepped to the fire and snatched the bottle from his hand.

"Plenty of time for that back at the bolt hole," Ben said, voice hard.

Ryderdale curled a lip but nodded.

"It'll be sun-up soon. We need the mules hitched to the wagons. And get Reyes to make sure the horses in the remuda are watered and fed and on a line," Ben said, voice louder, regaining command of the chaos.

"We're taking the wagons?" Ryderdale said.

"We're taking it all. When are we going to see a strike bigger than this? We sell off the load in Mexico and live like kings out of the Bible a while," Ben said.

"Here's to Solomon and all his gold!" a man said where he stood on the bench of a wagon.

"And all his wives," another said and raised a bottle in each hand. The men laughed at that, even the Mexicans who didn't understand the remark.

"Take a few healthy pulls, boys, then cork those bottles," Ben shouted to all. "We have work to do between here and dawn. We need clear heads. And we need to be well shy of this place before the sun gets high."

Joe looked to see men taking long slugs then slapping corks back in place in mute obedience. Ben Temple had seen them this far; they trusted his word and his mind to see them the rest of the way. The men fell to work hitching the teams while others went up into the rocks to bring down the horses the raiders had left on lines. Reyes was found and sent to prepare the remuda of horses for travel. Others moved among the dead, stooping to remove guns, holsters and any other valuables from the bodies lying about the camp. A few of these still clung to life and were finished off, amigos as well as strangers, with a knife to the throat or a rifle butt to the skull. It was a mercy to both. A wounded man didn't last long in this country. Even were a man to have a chance at surviving his injury, pity turned quickly to resentment among rough men on the trail. Better for all that they die sooner than later.

"What do you need me to do, Ben?" Joe asked.

"You done enough for one night, snakehand," Ben said, acknowledging the swiftness of young Joe's hand earlier.

Joe's eyes glittered over a shaky smile.

"Look around and find yourself some better irons, son," Ben said, patting Joe's shoulder as he stepped past him. "And a decent pair of boots before they're all taken."

Joe hared off to search the dead men. He came upon a man lying in the shadows under a wagon. A tall man dressed in dark clothes. Joe squatted down and took the man under the arms and dragged him into the glow of the firelight. The man wore a long black coat over a black vest. A gray-haired man with a long face and eyes staring red as rubies. A silver crucifix hung from a chain on his neck. Joe yanked it off and stuck it in a pocket of his shirt.

About the man's narrow hips was a holster rig of Spanish leather studded with brass rivets. A holster set with left-hand draw like the hand Joe favored. Mounted at a slant athwart the waist was a second holster for a smaller weapon. Joe unbuckled the belt and slid it off the man before crawling beneath the wagon for the guns it had held. He found a big Walker Colt in .44 and a slimmer Colt chambered to take a .32 ball.

He had to cinch the belt to the last hole in the loop before it would stay on his bony hips. The Walker weighed down on his left side to mid-thigh. The palm of his hand rested easy on the worn staghorn butt.

"Looks like a gun wearing a boy," Ryderdale scoffed. Some of the others guffawed. Joe raised his eyes to bore into the bigger man's, cold and hard. Ryderdale swallowed his smile and returned to help a couple men working to lift a wagon tongue from the ground for the approaching mule team.

"Snakehand," Joe said low in a whisper to himself. He tried a few pulls. The big Walker cleared the leather with an ease that felt natural as breathing.

From off in the dark came an agonized cry. Joe sniffed and his nose filled with the smell of burning fat and hair. The Indians were having their brand of fun with the survivors.

For the second time that day, Joe was grateful that there were no women among those on the wagons. He was surprised to find that, in addition to his left hand on the butt of the holstered Colt, his right was touching the pocket of his shirt in which the silver crucifix rested.

5

After having secured his new gun rig and liking the feel of it and the weight of his new firearm, Joe Wiley noted the quality of the coat the dead man at his feet wore. A heavy black preacher's frock coat. He kneeled and removed it from the corpse and stood back up with it draped from his hands. He inspected the garment. The blood would wash out easy enough with some scrubbing. It would serve him well to keep trail dust off during the day and stave off the chill of the desert night. Plus, he plain admired the look of it.

He noted a bullet in the left chest. He poked a finger into it and felt something inside. He flipped it around and dug into the inside pocket and produced a well-worn and much used Holy Bible. Bound in limp leather with pages trimmed in gold. The bible had stopped a bullet. Joe discovered the spent slug wedged well into the book. He pried it out with his fingers.

Joe had never properly learned to read, living like a scavenging coyote in his youth and following Ben around since then. No teachers or padres out in the wilderness to educate an unwanted child. Joe had always wanted to read and did try his hand at it every chance he had, to read signs or labels or whatever else had spelling on it. With Ben's help he could read maybe a hundred words. He looked down at the first page.

Joe read the words before him in a halting, uncertain meter.

"But… let… just… ice… roll… on… like… a river, right… ess… right…"

"Righteousness like a never-ending stream," Ben finished the verse from behind Joe.

Joe started, turning, and was embarrassed being caught reading so poorly. His face reddened and his dander got up.

"A body should be mindful of sneaking up on folks," Joe said.

Ben smiled easy. "Well, aren't we all a'bristle. I only thought I'd help you out. I see you found yourself the Good Book."

Joe looked down at his boots and then back up to the man who was only family he had ever known.

"Found it in my new coat. He must have been a preacher. I figured I'd start trying to read, I'm reckoning," Joe said and looked to Ben for a sign of approval.

"Good idea. Fine idea. This'll give you some good practice if nothing else. It sure was read a lot before now." Ben took the book and examined the well-read and worn pages. "Stopped a bullet even I see. But didn't stop the one that killed him." Ben slapped the book onto Joe's chest causing the younger man to clutch it.

"Never figured you for a man who read scripture," Joe said, his embarrassment giving way to a wry smile.

"Oh, I'm no holy man taken with religion. But there's words of wisdom in there. You can't go wrong with the lessons in there."

"Lessons about Moses and Jesus and like that?"

"Lessons about the human animal," Ben said

"What does right… righteousness mean, Ben?" Joe asked.

"It means doing good by yourself. Doing the right thing, the hard thing. It means being justified in what you do. That's what it means to me, anyhow."

"But what's it mean in the book?"

"It means carrying forward God's word through your deeds. Doing what He'd smile upon. It means Justice. Following His laws. Which isn't always the convenient way out here in hard country and hard times," Ben said.

Joe nodded and looked over at their fellow raiders working at the rewards of their attack. The teams were almost hitched. Reyes and a couple of Mexes were bringing the riding mounts out on lead lines.

"I mean to read this whole book. I mean to learn how to read good," Joe declared.

"You do that. And who knows you might find God while you're at it," Ben scolded Joe. "For sure though, that bible in your pocket and that big ass Walker on your bony hip presents an interesting paradox."

"What's paradox mean?" Joe asked.

"A contradiction. Two notions fighting each other. The bible or the gun. Death or righteousness. They don't ride easy together most times," Ben said.

That made Joe's brow knit as he stuffed the bible back into the coat pocket.

"Best get yourself cinched up. We'll be heading out soon," Ben said and clapped the youth on the shoulder.

Joe enjoyed the wordless gesture of approval and ran off to get his mount.

It was full morning by the time all the mule teams were hitched up to the wagons. The sunlight streaked through smoke from the guttering fire to reveal the still forms lying all around the campsite. All had been stripped of valuables, boots, weapons and clothing. The smell of cooked flesh hung in the bowl of land, rancid sweet smell of partly cooked tripe. It had the tang of pork to it, but all knew it wasn't swine.

Ben spoke to Muñoz from the saddle. The Mexican let out a long yelp and waved his sombrero over his head. Whips cracked, leather creaked and the big wheels on the teamster wagons broke out of the dusty ground to roll over the rocks and form up into a column.

The Comancheros began the long trek back to their hideout. In the end, ten of them had been lost in the fighting. The dead lay unburied and forgotten among the teamsters and pistoleros, amigos and enemies indistinguishable from one another. Food for the ants and birds.

But the raiders were now rich with blankets, guns, horses and other supplies from the teamsters and guards that they had killed. The best prize however was the government bonded whiskey that

Ben reckoned was intended as part payment for a treaty with the Kiowa up in Oklahoma Territory. He reckoned that that treaty and the absence of payment was the territorial governor's problem now. The whiskey would serve his and his men's purposes just fine and the peace betwixt the Kiowa and settlers be damned.

Ben rode over to where Joe was climbing onto the saddle of his own horse. He put out his hand to take the bridle and steady the roan for the younger man to swing a leg over. Ben's grin was broad and relaxed now that the deed was done, and they were heading on back to their hideaway. The boy looked a sight in the black coat and vest over buckskins and a soiled linen shirt.

"You want to ride lead with me a while, Snakehand?" Ben said once the boy was seated.

"If that's what you want, Ben," Joe said.

"Come ahead," Ben said and spurred his mount. They raced together along the line of wagons moving up an incline and out of the bowl of land. Through the pall of dust rising into the sky from the caravan a cloud of buzzards wheeled lower to fall on the bounty left behind.

They brought the stolen caravan into a pass after two days' ride. The narrow cleft in the high rock walls led to a densely wooded depression surrounded on all sides by defiles. The camp was made up of rough cabins in a grass clearing surrounding a good spring of fresh water. The men settled the wagons in a neat row on one end of the farthest cabin next to the horse pen. The men beat the dust from their clothing and set about making themselves back at home. The Indians had already broken from the rest and scurried off to their place in the outskirts of the area. None of them, not even Ben, knew where in the blind canyon they made camp.

"Son, this is just the beginning. We are building an empire. For the both of us. I'm going to be king of this entire territory and you can be its pope," Ben said and slapped Joe on the back. "All it takes is a little time, but we'll do it. Mark my words, son. I can see it all now." Ben swept his arms across the land before him.

Four weeks later the first man had died of the pox.

6

The Comanchero camp lay ghostly quiet but for the wind hissing in the pine tops.

Young Joe Wiley crouched by a pool dug before the spring opening. He filled two buckets with cold, fresh water and carried them, muscles aching, back toward the cabins. The horses and mules, set free to graze, parted before his approach.

Every man was down with one ailment or another. In the first days back to the camp, some of the men came down with stomach pains. Agonies that doubled them over and left them curled up and kicking on the ground with a terrible flux that loosened their bowels in stinking streams. These men died first. Ben Temple fell to this illness but was still among the living, thrashing like a wild thing in a bed fouled with his own wastes.

Others were afflicted with the pox, flesh hot to the touch and covered in running boils. Some were weak as kittens and lay struggling for each breath. Others were raving out of their minds and those were hardest to deal with. Joe had to bind them down to their bunks or bundle them in blankets to stop them wandering away.

Then there were the dead. Within two weeks half the camp was down with one complaint or another. There were hummocks of dirt in the pines where each lay in a shallow grave scraped from the sandy ground. Men died and finally Joe was the only one remaining on his feet and with all his wits. Joe was too occupied with saving men to bury any more of them. All he could do was haul them by the heels to a stack as far away from the cabins and the stream bed as his strength allowed. The pile was growing and beginning to stink even over the shit stench from the cabins. Flies covered the corpses in a boiling black cloud.

All the men who fell to the flux were dead now. All but Ben who lay in his cabin writhing like a soul in Hell until the pain made him faint dead away. There were eighteen left, white men and a few of the Mexicans. The Indians had been the first to slip away.

It was all Joe could do to keep the men from going dry. He'd give them drops of water squeezed from a cloth. He'd bathe them as best he could. He cut their filthy clothes away and burned them. They all lay naked now, shivering with eyes wide and frightened, seeing something beyond the confines of the log and mud walls around them. Joe would splash a bucket of water over them in hopes of quelling the fire that was consuming them from within.

He knew it was a losing fight. Every day he'd find one or more of the men lying still and cold, skin gone ashen, eyes like sun-parched pebbles in a dry wash. On the worst day he woke in the morning to find five men gone all at once.

The work was wearying and unforgiving. He'd taken to sleeping out of doors on a pine needle bed, grateful for the stiff wind coming down from the crest of rocks each evening. He might even take a few moments to sound out words from the bible: squinting in the firelight, running a dirty finger under each word.

"And Moses told these sayings unto all the children of Israel. And the people mourned greatly. And they rose up early in the morning and gat them up to the top of the mountain, saying, Lo, we will go up unto the place which the Lord hath promised for we have sinned."

Whether the Lord answered their prayers or not, Joe could not say as the next passages were lost in the ragged bullet hole burned through the page.

It seemed each time he lay down or closed his eyes he'd hear a call from one of the cabins and would rise to follow the voice to its source. Sometimes the man wanted water and sometimes he only wanted someone near, to not be alone.

These men who were murderers, thieves, and worse than those, turned to children under the cruel trials of the pox. They called for their mamas and, sometimes, believed that Joe was their mother. He would sit by them, even taking their burning hand in his, and listen to their pleas.

Ryderdale was one of the last to go and grabbed at Joe's arm with desperate strength.

"I done terrible deeds, boy. Terrible things I can't stop seeing," Ryderdale said. A man not much older than twenty years, his face was the face of an old man, wasted by illness, gray and drawn.

Joe tried to pull away, but the man clung to him, drawing him closer to the bed, his voice a dry croaking whisper.

"There was a girl, a real pretty girl, back in Rio Blanco. Her folks and mine went to the same meetings, the preacher's tent down by the river. She was awful pretty. Hair like…" The Texican was lost for the words to describe her further.

Joe tried to pry the man's hand from his arm but could not.

"She made sport of me. Called me a dumb turd and thought it was funny. She was so pretty, and I wanted her to like me real bad. I caught her on the river path once, all alone. I taught her not to make sport of me. Taught her I was damn sure good enough for the likes of her."

Joe surrendered to Ryderdale's grip, listening in silence to the man's confession.

"Couldn't have her telling no one so I bashed in her brain with rock. Dragged her into the rushes and left her there. Waded the Blanco and never came back. Never saw no one I ever knowed ever again. I done things. Terrible things. But that was most terrible of all."

His voice trailed away, mouth slack.

Joe sat on the edge of the bed until the hand gripping his arm relaxed and fell away. Joe hauled him from the bed and dragged the Texican out to drop him onto the growing pile of sinners who'd ridden the trail ahead of him to Perdition.

"Lo, we will go up unto the place which the Lord hath promised for we have sinned," he said to himself, walking from the stinking pile and back to the cabins where the remaining men groaned aloud for the only deliverance he could grant them.

The clearing was getting grazed out. It was never meant to provide feed for so many mounts. Their own ponies, along with the mules and the horses they'd stolen, were chewing the grass down to bare dirt. Joe penned up Ben's pinto mare along with a couple of other ponies. He mounted his roan and fired three rounds from the Walker into the air. The blasts had the horses up and milling. Waving a blanket in his hand, he herded the horses out through the trees and into the pass. Most of the mules trotted after. He rode drag, whooping and swinging the blanket over his head until the bulk of the herd was out through the pass and back into open country where they'd be free to find feed and water on their own.

He reined in the roan atop a shelf of rock and watched the mounts and drays canter away over a rise and out of sight in a smoke of yellow dust. Joe closed his eyes and raised his head to take in what felt like the first clean breath of air he'd had in a month. It smelled of cedar and sage. The sun warmed his face. For a fleeting second, he felt a rush, an urge to spur the roan down to follow the now renegade herd to the north and leave the pesthole of death and despair and low men far behind him.

Then he remembered that Ben Temple was still alive. Joe wheeled the roan around and headed back into the shadows of the pass at a walk. He meant to enjoy the ride as long as it lasted.

The following day saw the last of the raiders pass away. Joe left them where they lay in their sick beds and stepped from the cabin to see Ben Temple walking away in the sunshine in an unsteady gait, his Enfield rifle in his hands. Joe rushed to him and steadied him, helping Ben to a seat on a fallen log set by the cook fire for that purpose. He spoke low to Ben as he guided him to the fire.

"Get me a drink of water, son," Ben said in reply and Joe rushed to the spring with a bucket.

Ben drank long and greedy from the bucket and handed it back and made a sweeping gesture.

Joe fetched a second bucket. Ben took it and upended it over his head. The ice-cold water splashed over his naked body, sluicing away weeks of accumulated filth.

"Who's left?" Ben said, blowing water out of his mustache and beard as he spoke. He was gaunt now from the ravages of the illness and loss of weight. But his voice was regaining its commanding timbre.

"You and me, Ben. That's all. I just let most of the horses go free," Joe said, and Ben nodded.

"It was the blankets or maybe the liquor," Ben said. A shaking hand found Joe's shoulder; the fingers squeezed.

"What are you saying?"

"I've heard of it before. Blankets full of pox. Whiskey tainted with poison. Those wagons might as well as had the Grim Reaper sitting on the drivers' boxes."

"You said they were part of a treaty, Ben."

"I said I thought as much. And they may well have been. Only no treaty the government ever meant to keep. This devil's freight was meant for the Kiowas, sure. Meant to kill them every buck, squaw and child," he said and dropped his hand from Joe's shoulder.

"Damnation," Joe breathed.

"Didn't drink as much of that brew as the others. Never been a souse. Glad of it now, I guess," Ben said, head lowered, hand to his face.

"You guess? Well, you're alive, ain't you?" Joe said, laughing.

"That I am that, Snakehand," Ben said and turned his face to Joe, a grim smile showing through his beard, eyes glassy.

"And blind as a bat on a moonless midnight."

7

The locomotive stood along the long platform of roughhewn timber, sending a tower of white smoke into a cloudless sky of pearlescent blue. It was huffing like a horse panting for the waters of a cooling stream. The freshly white-washed water tower stood just beyond the station house. The name of the town was painted in neatly spaced crimson letters either side.

Mercury Wells.

The wells outside of town being the entire reason for the town's being. Deep springs that delivered the needed water to a thirsty railroad at the promised speed of Mercury himself. The town itself looked just born or perhaps sprung up out of the land overnight.

Only a half dozen of the buildings down the main strip sported paint. The rest were bare wood, some with shake roofs. Even more were covered with tarred canvas. Tents were in abundance. The boardwalks were still under construction in anticipation of winter rains that would turn the wide main street into a sea of muck. But for now, under the hammering sun of summer, the place was dry as old bones. There was a single structure of brick that sat midway between the finished buildings and the lanes of tents beyond. It was low and flat roofed and formed a dividing line between newcomers and the newly established as certain as a wall of Jericho.

A slim man, dressed all in black from head to silver-tipped toes, stepped from a passenger car onto the platform. He wore a pair of Colts in an unusual left-handed rig. His coat was jet black and long. A fine gold chain hung across his vest and from it dangled a tiny crucifix in silver. His hair was silver as well, worn longish and brushed back to touch his collar under a broad-brimmed black Stetson with a flat crown.

He stood a moment in silent appraisal of the train station and the town beyond. Porters were working to unload freight from a mail car and, farther down the rails, a ramp was being brought up to a horse cart. The man in black squinted to a boy squatting in the shadows of the station awning. He fished in a pocket and brought out a half-dollar coin and held it for the boy to see. The boy, a half-breed with a filthy face and ragged clothes, raced over to the man, eyes on the coin glinting in the sun.

"See that chestnut mare they're bringing out?" the man said.

The boy looked to see a horse stamping its feet on the ramp as a porter led it down on the dirt alongside the tracks. The boy nodded.

"Her name is Sassafras. You bring her and her saddle along to the livery. Then come find me at the hotel."

"Which hotel, mister?"

"Which is the best hotel, son?"

"The Grand Prairie."

"Then find me at the Grand Prairie," the man said and dropped the half-dollar into the boy's open hand.

"Who I ask for?" the boy said, staring at the most money he'd ever held in his hand in his life.

"Joe Wiley," the man said.

The boy looked up, his prize forgotten, to goggle open-mouthed at the tall stranger. Then, clutching the coin, he ran off to where the porter stood holding the reins of the chestnut mare.

"What's it look like, son?" said a man stepping from the car to the head of the steps. The man wore gray whiskers streaked with white but neatly trimmed. He wore smoked lenses on his face under a battered hat. His clothes were fine gray wool but rumpled from the long trip. He gripped a carpet bag in a gloved hand.

"Like any other tank town," Joe Wiley said and reached a hand up to the older man, only to have it batted away.

"Smells like a cow town."

"There's beef all right."

"How many steps?" Ben Temple asked in irritation.

"Three and a drop," Joe said with a crooked smile, lowering his hand.

One hand gliding lightly on the handrail, Ben moved down to hop to the platform.

"You Joe Wiley?" A man crossed the platform with a hand out. Two men followed him as if towed on a line. All three were drovers, hard men in hats with busted brims, patched shirts and chaps worn over boots with worn heels. Gloves with flared cuffs were folded in the belt straps of their chaps. The man in the lead walked and moved like a boss, a Schofield revolver hung in a Mexican rig at his hip. The other two weren't heeled though one held a Sharps carbine cradled in his arms. It was Joe's livelihood to notice things like that.

"Homer Gibbs," the boss man said. "Ramrod and foreman from the Three Rivers."

"It was your employer who wired me," Joe said taking the man's hand in his. A hard callused hand, white across the back with the scars of old rope burns.

"I was over running some stock in and saw the train coming in. Thought maybe you'd be on it as Mr. Nostrand's been expecting you this week." Gibbs nodded across the tracks to the high fences and cowsheds of a stockyard set away from the rail line.

"Thanks for the welcome. Will I be seeing Mr. Nostrand?"

"Not for a few days, I'd figure. He told me to keep a look out for you. He wanted you to have this in the meanwhile." Gibbs retrieved a leather sack from a pocket of his vest and held it out. Joe noticed it was tied with a length of steel wire.

"And what is this?" Joe took the sack and weighed it in his hand.

"Mr. Nostrand said to tell you to consider it a sort of advance in exchange for taking up his offer," Gibbs said, eyeing the sack with a look of veiled curiosity that let Joe know that he had not looked in the sack himself.

"Well, thank him for me and tell him I look forward to meeting him myself," Joe said, placing the sack in the pocket of his coat.

Gibbs nodded and grunted in reply before he and the silent pair backed away to step from the platform and cross the tracks back to the yards.

"I hear a jingle," Ben said, stepping to Joe's side as they stepped away from the train.

"You heard the man. An advance," Joe said and walked a half pace before his friend.

"Sounded like gold coins. Gold makes a warmer sibilance than silver when it clinks," Ben said.

"One step," Joe said, and Ben made the single step from the timber platform to the hard pan without a second's hesitation in his progress.

"In advance of what exactly?" Ben said.

"Certain considerations, I would wager."

Ben snorted.

"That's what I thought," Joe said as the pair made their way from the station and down the bustling main drag of yet another boomtown needing the hand of a righteous man.

8

Joe Wiley and Ben Temple made their way down the partly constructed boardwalk. Joe kept an eye on the older man just in case, even if the need was a rare thing. The man was sure-footed, adjusted to his world of private darkness. Many folks met him, even spent time with him, unaware that he was sightless.

They walked past the usual variety of establishments found in new-born towns like Mercury Wells. A mercantile, a bank, an apothecary, dollar stores, a hostelry or two, a big cook tent, and saloons. Lots of saloons. Painted across their broad fronts was a promise of cold beer, fine liquor and fair tables. There would be women too, but propriety forbade advertising that brazen even in a wild settlement like this.

More civilization creeping into the west, Joe thought, or what passes for civilization in cow country.

There was some wagon traffic on the street and saddle horses and rigs hitched before the shops and saloons. People moved in the shade of the boardwalks. Sullen nesters with tired looking wives and dirty children in tow. The nesters looked about with their heads on swivels, eyeing the world through suspicious eyes. Men in fine clothes and shiny shoes sat smoking cigars on perambulating chairs under the awning before a saloon. Cowhands stood leaning on hitching posts, watching the street and exchanging remarks. Mexican vaqueros sat on benches along the wall of an alley between buildings, passing a clay jug and smoking rolled cigarettes. Some

Chinese were chattering to one another in their sing-song tongue as they worked clothes in washtubs of steaming lye water before a laundry tent. A huckster stood before a dollar store speaking to everyone and no one, inviting the world inside to view his wares.

The population would grow after dark. This town would rise up then and kick the gong until sunrise. Joe could tell that by the number of saloons lining the street. It was simple arithmetic. A whole lot of liquor and too few whores to go around.

Joe turned them toward a shingle announcing The Grand Prairie Hotel. They crossed the dusty street to reach a building larger than its neighbors. It was certainly grand in comparison to the rest of the structures along the drag. Fresh paint on the boards, the name of the hotel written in fancy swirling crimson letters trimmed in gilt. A shake roof above a wide veranda off a second and third floor. Brass lanterns hung from red-painted porch rails. The place stood out like a jewel in the half-built camp town spreading out around it either side of the main street like a spill.

Joe and Ben made their way through glass-paneled doors into the lobby where they were immediately greeted by the front man, a ruddy-faced fellow with hair, brush mustache and mutton chops of coppery red.

"Welcome, gentlemen! Will ye be needin' a room then?" the clerk asked eagerly.

"For quite a bit actually, if all goes well," Joe answered. "You take monthly rental?"

"Certainly, sir! My name is Hamish MacDougal. You may call me Ham, as everyone who knows me does. I run this modest hostel."

"Fine looking house. You stand to do well by yourself as this town grows," Joe said. "I'm Joe Wiley. This is Ben Temple."

"One hopes, sir. One hopes," Ham said, and skirted around the desk to take his place at the register. "That is certainly the plan, sir. I have a very nice suite upstairs. Or are you wanting adjoining rooms?"

"What a waste," Ben snorted.

"We'll take adjoining rooms. He snores like a mud-stuck bull. A boy will be along with our things. Send him up when he gets here. What do I owe you?"

"Twenty dollars, monthly rate. The place across the road has the best meals in town and charges half again too little for them," Ham suggested. "I'll show you to your room."

Joe nodded. He and Ben followed Ham who took the stairs two at a time.

"Eight steps and a turn to the right. Five more to the top," Joe said for Ben alone. Ben grunted in reply, one hand lightly tapping the banister. They reached the third floor to find Ham holding a door for them. There were doors to four rooms. Two suites of two adjoined rooms, Joe reckoned.

Ham gave them a tour of the rooms as Ben made his way about the room he'd chosen as his own, laying fingers on a dresser top, bed posts, a water pitcher on a dry sink. He was memorizing the room's dimensions and the objects in it. He reached the windows to find large sash casement windows, three panels set in a wooden frame. The tips of his fingers played over panes and found them laced with muntins in a diamond shaped pattern. He stood feeling the sun on his face through the panes of cut glass, a hand running down the edge of lace curtains. Ham watched with mounting umbrage.

"I assure you, sir, you'll find your room cleaner than any other you'd find in this town," Ham said, chest swollen and nose raised.

"I can see that. Clean as a dog's ass," Ben said, taking the man's meaning. "Only admiring these windows."

Ham smiled with pride. "You've taken notice of my Queen Anne's. A bit of bonnie Scotland in my new home in Texas."

"I don't supposed you have any 'bonnie' Scotch around your new home?" Ben said, winking a blind eye.

"The Grand does not, as yet, hold a license to sell liquor. But a wee dram between friends is within the law, am I right?" Ham grinned.

"I believe the law will abide a drink or two," Joe said, stepping through the companion door between the rooms. He made his way to the windows that fronted on the street. He parted the curtains to look down on the town below. This was the highest place around, Mercury Wells sitting on land as flat as a pan.

"You can practically see the entire town from these windows. Quite a view," Ham said in the doorway.

"And a balcony as well." Joe swung a window open to lean out. There were a few wooden chairs sitting out on the planks. He looked forward to sitting there of an evening, watching the sun set over the distant horizon. More than that, it was high ground. A man, a man who knew what to look for, could learn a lot from this vantage point.

"Will there be anything else, sirs?" Ham said.

"Where might I find the mayor this time of the day?" Joe asked.

"He has a fine house on the north end of town. But at this hour I'd swear he'd be at the post office. He's postmaster here as well," Ham said.

"I'll be back once I've met him. Give this to the boy when he gets here with our goods. And this one is for you," Joe said, taking Ham's beefy hand and dropping two dollar coins into his palm.

"That I'll do, sir," Ham said and, with a curt bow, took his leave.

"Well, what do you think?" Joe said when they were alone.

"It'll do. I ain't tried the mattress yet," Ben said and stooped to rest his behind on the edge of the bed.

"About the town," Joe said, a smile on his mouth, knowing the older man understood precisely what he was asking about.

"I smell money under the cow shit, son," Ben said with a sigh as he lay back on the bed, rocking his shoulders to work into a comfortable place.

9

The U.S. post office was one of the few brick buildings in town. It had a roof of tin metal sheet and tiny windows braced with iron bars. Strands of telegraph wire ran to it from the station house along a row of poles set behind the buildings on the north side of the main street. The front and rear doors were propped open to allow for a breeze.

Two men stood in the lobby area playing a game of checkers on a board resting atop a pile of wooden crates. An older man with steel gray hair, thick around the middle, in shirtsleeves and a vest worn open. The other was leaner, taller, in a loose blouse and whipcord trousers. Hair pomaded and parted in the middle. Joe took note of the revolver hanging low on the man's thigh. A third man watched the game with indifference, a flay pipe clamped in his lips. This man was slight with sloping shoulders, eyeglasses fixed on a chinless face atop a wattled neck.

At the desk window Joe asked after the mayor.

"And who may I ask is calling?" said the man at the window cage. A man in shirt sleeves held up by garters, a wrinkled ribbon tie, a plug hat on his head. He had the saddest eyes Joe had ever seen, pearly blue and wet like a hound's, framed by a salt-and-pepper beard and sideburns.

"Joe Wiley. I believe he's expecting me."

"Welcome to Mercury Wells, Mr. Wiley," the man at the desk said, his demeanor brightening, a hand shooting out through the gate in the window to shake Joe's. "Mayor Geoffrey Tuchman. I hope your trip here wasn't too onerous."

"A train ride is pleasant in comparison to sitting a saddle that distance," Joe said.

"As well it might. Yes, sir," the mayor said and slipped on a coat with silk lapels. He opened a gate in the cage to take Joe by the arm. He gestured to the men about the checkerboard. "These men are my colleagues and fellow town fathers. Our banker Ned Merriweather."

"Greetings," Merriweather said, the chinless man giving a sharp darting of his head which caused his slicked back hair to flick slightly and his wattle to sway.

"Our railroad man from Southwest General, Tom Blankenship." The chunky man stood and extended a hand.

"Welcome to Mercury Wells," said the man as he took Joe's hand with a firm grip. Joe saw now that Blankenship had steely eyes to go with his hair, and the complexion of a man who has worked outside more often than not. Joe reckoned the man had worked as a railroad man before he became the boss of one. His hand, still rough from old calluses, was proof of that.

"Based on my ride here you run a fine train," Joe said.

The mayor said, "And our County Constable Bob Miller. The two of you will be working together the most."

"Hello," said Miller. The youngest man here and someone Joe could immediately see was an ambitious sort who meant to be someone sooner rather than later. The tie-down gunfighter rig and the narrowed eyes told Joe all he needed to know.

"I reckon so," Joe agreed and shook Miller's hand. He didn't have the iron grip of Blankenship, but not for a lack of trying.

"Have a seat so we can dicker out this whole thing," Mayor Tuchman said. "And smoke yourself one of these." Tuchman produced what Joe could tell was a fine cigar from a silver holder he'd fished from an inside pocket of his coat.

"Don't mind if I do." Joe took the offered cigar. He took a seat in an empty chair. Blankenship produced a match and lit the corona for Joe.

Joe relaxed in the comfortable leather chair and took a few puffs.

"We asked you here, Mr. Wiley, because our new town has a problem. Not a problem that is unique to us by any means, but a problem, nevertheless. And it is the sort of problem you have a reputation for being very good at sorting out," Tuchman said.

"Drifters. Sharpers. Wild cowboys. Mexicans. All sorts of ill repute have descended on us. We need some order," Blankenship said.

"We want to build something here. A place where we can raise families," Merriweather said, eyes intense behind his bottle-glass lenses.

A place where you can make yourselves a shit-pile of money, Joe thought.

Joe nodded. "That's a sure common problem, all right. Common as dirt."

"As I stated in my wire, we mean to hire you as our town marshal. We'll need you to bring this town to heel, save it from going to hell before it has a chance at a future. We stand to lose a lot of money if our plans are ruined or even stalled," the mayor said.

"I imagine so," Joe said, taking a long pull on the cigar and allowing a thin stream of blue smoke to fan out over the low ceiling.

"And it's worth a lot to protect those plans, am I right?" Joe said to the men, each for their own reasons anxious to hear his ideas on the matter at hand.

"Of course. We asked around for the best. Your name kept coming up. Nostrand out at the Three Rivers suggested we contact you. We're in a tight spot here, Mr. Wiley. Tell us what it will take to bring you to Mercury Wells," the railroad man said, tapping the top of the crate with a finger causing the pieces on the checkerboard to clatter about.

Joe sat forward to lean elbows on the crate, the cigar between steepled fingers before him. The men leaned in, all but Miller who remained upright, keeping his distance and his eyes hooded.

"I need room and board at the Grand Prairie for me and my… associate. Any expenses incurred while serving the law will be covered by the town. Livery costs, ammunition and other sundries. Plus, two hundred dollars a month and a fifty dollar bonus for each conviction," Joe said.

The men sat silent and drank in Joe's proposal. All but Miller.

"My ass!" Miller sputtered, kicking back his chair as he stood. "How do you reckon you're worth so much?"

"Which saloon is the worst in town?" Joe asked the room, ignoring the constable's outburst.

"The Paradise. It's a bucket of blood," Merriweather answered. His voice quivered at the mention of the place.

"Have a contract drawn up to my stated specifications and a month's payment when I get back," Joe said, rising from his seat.

Joe left the post office, Miller on his heels.

"Well, you have to admit, the man has sand," the mayor said.

10

The Paradise was anything but.

There were gunshots sounding from inside the Paradise even as Joe followed the boardwalk toward the simple shingle with the saloon's name painted on it in crude letters. Below it hung a cloth banner promising nickel shots.

Unpainted plank walls nailed up on half-timber posts formed the walls. The roof was stretched tent canvas. The street front was wide open under an awning. The only attempt at decoration was a sagging string of pennants across the opening with the Stars and Stripes and the Lone Star flag hanging limp and faded.

The place stunk of sweat, tobacco and beer gone skunky.

The floor was sand and sawdust. The bar was just a broad plank resting atop barrels. There were no chairs on which to sit. Men stood and drank until they chose to leave or could no longer stand. The only table was set across the back where a dealer operated a wheel under the uncertain light of oil lamps. The field of numbers were painted atop the sanded surface in red and black. In addition to the dealer, the game was watched by a dour looking man seated on a high stool with a cut-down coach gun across his knees. The man was the size of a mountain, broad of girth with pig eyes under a sloped brow.

Joe stood under the awning, taking in the smell and noise as his eyes adjusted to the light. Bob Miller was at his elbow close enough that Joe could smell his brand of chaw.

His eyes swept the room to where three cowboys were tossing shot glasses in the air, taking turns shooting at them with revolvers. One would make the throw and the other two would plug away. The crowd whooped and laughed and yelled for more. The glasses either dropped to strike the heads of fellow customers or fell to the sand floor unscathed. The trio of drovers was only managing to shoot holes in the canvas above them. The bartenders, rough-looking fellows in stained aprons, seemed to show no concern at the giggling drunks shooting up the glassware and ceiling.

Joe parted the half-ring of onlookers and stepped through a wreath of gun smoke to approach the three at the bar. Bob Miller slipped away to watch from a safe distance.

"That's enough for now, boys," Joe said, smiling easy.

The three turned to him, eyes bleary and lacking focus. Their audience shifted their attention from the shooting contest to this newcomer in the preacher's coat.

The drovers smirked and turned from Joe to return to their game. One of them bent an arm back to toss a new shot glass. The other two stood, eyes skyward, revolvers cocked in their fists.

Joe hooked the thrower's elbow and levered the man off his feet to strike the back of his head on the edge of the oak plank that served as a bar top. The other two turned too late, guns leveled. Joe reached them in a single stride, stepping over their friend, and snatched the pistols from their grasps. Before they could react to their suddenly empty hands, Joe had brought the butts of the guns down on their heads. Both men dropped as though suddenly boneless, one on his ass, the other to his knees.

The metallic click of a drawn hammer caused Joe to spin, the pair of borrowed pistols, hammers already drawn back, whirled in his hands. He fired off both guns at the glass-thrower, now raising himself up to one knee, his Colt coming up to train on Joe as the twin bullets struck him in the chest inches apart.

The drover was thrown back against a keg hard enough to tip bottles off the bar top then lay still, a dark stain spreading over his filthy shirt.

Joe straightened, thumbing back the hammers of the pistols once more as his eyes traveled across the room. The ring of men had broken up and retreated well back, mouths agape. The bartenders had taken a step away from the bar top. One held a sawn-off pick handle in his fist but swiftly dropped it when Joe's eyes fell on him. The dealer had ducked beneath his wheel. The big man on the stool sat motionless; the shotgun on his knees remained in place. His only look-out was the wheel and the table—the death of some dumb cowboy meant nothing to him.

"Miller," Joe said, and saw the county constable stepping between two goggle-eyed customers.

"You're my witness," Joe said to the constable, handing him the pair of borrowed pistols.

"Witness to what?" Miller said, voice catching then recovering himself.

"That's my first conviction," Joe said, nodding to the dead man turning ashen gray in a pool of sodden red sand.

"And those two?" Miller said of the other two drovers stirring and moaning on the dirty floor. He stuck the pistols in his waistband then stooped to pick up the dropped Colt.

"I don't happen to have any deputies, do I?"

"You do not."

"Then you can help me with the other pair. And lead the way. I don't know where my jail is yet," Joe said.

Miller did as he asked and they had the dazed drovers out the door, shoved by the collar back in the direction of the post office.

"No need to add that fracas to my expenses," Joe said, weaving through the growing crowd of gawkers drawn to the spectacle.

"Add what?" Miller said, confused.

"The bullets. I didn't use any of my own back there," Joe said.

11

Ben Temple sawed off another bite of the aromatic and juicy steak placed before him. He stabbed the hunk of meat with his fork and lifted it to his face, breathing in the enticing smell of the charbroiled morsel before taking it into his mouth. He made sounds of pleasure as he masticated the flavorful, moist, and perfectly cooked cow flesh.

"Good isn't it?" Joe Wiley smiled over his own plate filled with a slab of beef.

"I'll grant you that Scotchman didn't lie about it. Slow cooked and properly marinated. Cooking longhorns is an art, and this is an artist at work, son," Ben said, chewing.

Joe nodded as he hungrily tucked into his steak.

The dining room of the Grand Prairie was, as expected, as well appointed as the rest of the hotel. The lower walls and the furnishings done in the Queen Anne style like the rest of the place. Worldly elegance with a soft and light mien. The emphasis on appearance and comfort. The tables and chairs had a graceful curvilinear form and were marked by cabriole legs, the chair backs comfortably curved to fit the spine and crowned by a simple carved shell. All the pieces were crafted from mahogany and embellished with lacquered detailing and displayed a reddish polished sheen. Someone has put some money and taste as well as pride into this oasis.

Ben and Joe felt like kings on their thrones in some fine dining hall of old.

"The only thing that would be better is if I could listen to some fine music after a stomach full of meat and some quality belly wash," Ben said.

"Bound to be somewhere that'll provide that pleasure," Joe said. "Among others."

At that moment the hotel waiter, a man of short stature who, by divine providence, was named Little and, adding insult to injury, dubbed Shorty from early on, came to check on his charges and refill their drinking glassware.

"Everything satisfactory, gents?"

"Couldn't be better. Except for finishing up with some good music and a stiff drink afterwards. Where would a body find that in Mercury Wells?" Ben asked.

"The Majestic. It's got a pipe organ and the smoothest drinks this side of the Pecos," Shorty said.

"Thank you kindly. That will add to your gratuity. That sounds just the place. A home away from home." Ben smiled easy, wiping his chin with a white linen napkin.

"Or just a home. The other place is just the place to sleep it off," Joe said. He smirked and gave a wink at Shorty. Shorty winced a smile back and returned to his work.

"Well at least the new town marshal will know where to find me," Ben said.

"I never needed to be a marshal to know that," Joe said.

"Well, I did some listening around. As I do often. My eyes may be useless, but these ears pick up a lot. You sit long enough, and folks ignore your presence, let their mouths run. And what I have heard tells me this town is a snake pit. Lots of money and no direction or real order. Everybody out for himself. That is a very dangerous combination. Particularly for someone that is out to change that in any significant way. You step careful, marshal," Ben warned.

Joe listened to the older man and weighed his words with respect and sobriety. Joe nodded.

"I'll be as careful as I need to be and still get the job done," Joe said.

"This town's got powerful men with interests here. Lot of cash on the table. Some of their interests are shared. Cattlemen need the railroad and railroads need freight. Cowboys need a place to get their bells rung and a gutful of whiskey. That's where your work is."

"Different town. Same old story. The moneymen want a balance of peace and profit. I'm that balance, Ben."

"But there's something else here. Can't you feel it? This town under six months old but here we sit in a hotel as fine as anything in Austin or even New Orleans. That's money. Bigger money than a shithole town like this deserves. Hell, you and I both know this Mercury Wells will be a ghost town inside of five years. Maybe less," Ben said, leaning over the table, voice low.

Joe shrugged. "The Scotchman overplayed his hand. Spent his money unwisely."

"Hell. That Scotty didn't build this place. Ever see a Hibernian throw around money like this? He's just a hired man. Someone else paid a pile to set this up. Probably has money spent all over the county."

"The railroad, maybe?"

"They got what they want here already. A water stops and a railhead for beeves. No, son. It's something else."

"You keep your ear to the ground then, old man," Joe said.

"What's your first step here?" Ben said, tilting sweet cream into his coffee.

"I'll be needing deputies. I've already sent wires out for some able guns. But no reply as yet. I told Coolie Taylor to join us here. No word back."

"I'll be able to smell that one when he hits town," Ben cracked wise.

"One way or the other, I will have the reins on Mercury Wells inside a month. Maybe sooner," Joe said.

Ben nodded, face solemn. Their dinner conversation was disrupted by the shriek of a woman from somewhere nearby.

Joe stood abruptly and kicked back his chair to dash out of the hotel.

Shorty ran to the door to see what he could see of the commotion on the lamp-lit street.

"He's like one of those old Knights of the Round-table. He hears a woman cry and he is off like a shot," Ben said. "Now, what does your menu offer for dessert, Shorty?"

12

Joe Wiley ran out into the wide dusty main road of Mercury Wells and quickly determined that the screams were coming from the Paradise. The roar of men's voices rose to match the volume of a woman's shrieks.

He arrived at the saloon to find a gang of rough types, crusted with the dirt and funk of many miles on the trail, crushed against the bar. They had a young whore standing up atop the plank. She was naked save for her garters. She had a face that was still pretty though a few more months selling herself would change that. A spray of freckles across a face framed by ginger red hair. She was slim with spindly legs, narrow hips and mere buds for breasts. But a sight for sore eyes for men who had been out on the range for months eating dust and staring at the ass-end of a world of beeves.

The space under the canvas was crowded with patrons but it was easy enough to see that the filthy pack of drovers was the center of the chaos. Though the customers were watching with amusement, not a one lifted a hand to help the terrified girl balanced upon the bar top. The roulette table at the back was unoccupied. The man with the shotgun was gone, his high stool empty.

A bartender lay still on the floor, his head bleeding. Another stood backed to the wall, scared out his mind he would end up like his co-worker. The same one who held up a pick handle to Joe earlier. All bluff gone now.

Joe cut the shot caller out of the bunch at first glance. A big bastard in chaps with silver conchos. He was swiping a buck knife at the whore's ankles, making her dance. Her clothes—dress, slip and bustier—lay in the filthy sand where the cowhands had sliced them from her. She bled freely from a nick over her ribs where some rowdy's hand slipped in the work of cutting. The big man and his saddle trash comrades crowded the bar to watch.

"Dance sweet for me, you skinny bitch!" the big man shouted.

The girl was terrified and trying her damnedest to dance. She was making a poor show of it, body trembling and feet shuffling like a sleepwalker. Tears streamed down her face turning the lamp black on her lashes into ebon rivulets down her cheeks.

"Let that girl be," Joe said, parting the men as he neared the bar front.

The big man turned to face Joe, looking him up and down with a sneer. The wicked blade of the knife flashed in his hand.

"And why should I? Who're you to tell me anythin'?" the big man sneered. His eyes were mean with drink. Probably started out mean. Whiskey only built a fire under his evil nature.

"Because I am the law and I said so," Joe said.

"Kill that sunvabitch," the big man said with casual ease and turned his attention back to the girl trembling on the bar.

Two of the saddle tramps went for their guns. Even before they cleared the holsters, they lay on the ground dead from Joe Wiley's gun. One bullet for each drilled through their chests.

The sudden fury of the violence silenced the celebration. The big man and his gang moved off the bar to circle Joe with wild anger and murderous intent in their eyes. The rest of the bar patrons receded like oil on water, stepping back to observe what promised to be the main entertainment of the evening.

Joe braced, back to the bar, both Colts in his fists. The hammers were drawn back. He picked out the first two who would die. After that he'd play it as it rolled.

"You get down now, girl," Joe said, voice cool, to the whore still balanced atop the bar. He felt the plank atop the barrels buck against the back of his coat as she climbed down.

The ring of men coiled about him like a serpent prepared to strike but weighing its options. Most mobs would have dissolved by now, what with two of their number lying on the sand bleeding out. Only these drovers had enough liquor in them to get a bulge on and keep it. They had this lawman outnumbered ten to one. Those were good odds. But surely one or more of them would get plugged in the rush before they brought the bastard down. Those odds were not so sweet.

Strong drink has a way of blurring a man's calculations, making him believe that he won't be that unlucky. Joe Wiley could see it in the eyes of the men seething around him. They were building to make their move. He could only stand and wait for it.

Behind the phalanx of cowhands Joe saw the onlooking crowd of bar patrons parting like the Red Sea before Moses himself. Murmurs and chatter rose but one distinct voice called out.

"Let me through!"

And a beautiful woman dressed all in white, corn silk hair pinned to the back of her head in a net, emerged through the drunken drovers to stand before them, facing Joe. The woman was like an avenging angel, face severe with a rage that did nothing to mar her lovely features. If anything, to Joe's estimation, her open emotions made her all the more attractive.

"Stop! Stop this instant!" she commanded.

13

"Have you not the shame God gave every man? Have you not the sense God gave a wood tick?" the woman said, her eyes sweeping the circle of men, including the new town marshal. She was spitting mad. Joe noted for the first time that she held a length of cane in her delicately gloved hand. She cut at the drovers with the cane, sweeping it back and forth. It cut the air with a whistling sound. The cowboys took a step back, the prospect of this wildcat female slashing their faces with a cane end bringing them to a moment of sobriety.

A dozen or so women joined her, coming through the gap made in the ranks by the white-clad hellion like a host of seraphs riding into hell. The cowboys and the other patrons made way for them. These were more common angels, sturdy women in dull dress with faces made ugly with righteous rage. Each was armed with a length of cane.

"Is it not enough you drink and smoke and chew more like beasts than men? Is it not enough that you defile female flesh with your base animal desires? But you must hasten your damnation, assure your torment in the realm eternal, by further humiliating a fallen woman?" The woman in white admonished every swinging dick within earshot.

She made her way past Joe to step behind the bar, stepping over the fallen bartender and elbowing the other aside. The adminis-

tering angel lifted the trembling whore from where she crouched behind a barrel. Her hands to the girl's shoulders.

"Are you a peace officer, sir?" the woman said. Joe didn't realize at first that she was addressing him. His attention was still on the surrounding press of men now held at bay by the company of women suddenly in their midst.

"I am, ma'am," Joe said, not turning, Colts held unwavering on the big bastard with the buck knife still in his fist.

"May I have your coat to cover this poor, despoiled child?" the woman asked, though it was clear she expected his full cooperation.

"That may be awkward as I'm at what you might call an impasse here, ma'am."

"Sisters," the woman said.

Without further command, the crew of women stepped between the bar and the goggling mob of patrons. They stood like a bristling hedge between Joe and the drovers. The largest of them, a broad-beamed matronly type, whipped her cane through the air. The drunks recoiled, taking a stumbling step back.

Joe holstered his .36 and slipped an arm from his coat. He switched the larger Colt to his right hand with a flickering motion. He slipped the coat free and held it out behind him.

"Perhaps you'd like to accompany us from here?" the angel said.

"Move to the door. I'll be covering you," Joe said and restored the smaller Colt to his left hand and trained both on the shifting mob of drovers. The barricade of women filed toward the tent opening behind their leader who was taking the young whore out to the street, Joe's coat wrapped about her.

Joe waited until the women were clear and backed toward the opening. His guns trained steady on the cowboys. The big honcho eyeballed him with mean pig-eyes.

"You heard the lady bringing you the word of God," Joe said as he retreated out of the lamp light into the dark of the street. "But I will be back in here shortly and it'll be the devil himself coming with me."

Joe trotted after the group of women making their way along the street toward the back of town. He reached the woman in white who walked at the lead, her arm about the young whore. She was speaking low to the girl, comforting words. Joe walked alongside the woman and her young charge without speaking. The entourage made its way past saloons filled with the sounds of roaring men and cackling women. From the belly of the Majestic came the rumbling tones of a pump organ. Pimps stood before their tents extoling passing men with the virtues of the women waiting within in terms that made up in frankness what they lacked in imagination. Two drunks were engaged in a pathetic excuse for a fist fight in the mud before a horse trough.

"You sure turned the herd back there, ma'am," Joe said at last.

"I only wish I'd arrived earlier, marshal. Those two unfortunate men would still be alive," she said, eyes forward.

"That pair made their choice, ma'am. It was by my hand but *out* of my hands, if you take my meaning."

"We are all in God's hands, sir."

"And that same God gave us choice. It's what separates us from the beast of the field. If you'll excuse the contradiction, ma'am."

She looked to him for the first time, a look of cold appraisal. Impossible to tell from her frozen expression what judgement she'd made of him.

"Might I suppose you follow only to see your coat returned?" She sniffed.

"I thought to see you and your sisters to safety, ma'am. My duty as a peace officer."

"The Lord will see us home, marshal."

"The name is Joe Wiley."

She glanced at him again. Eyes flashing green. Was that the start of a smile he saw for a fleeting second?

"Sister Adeline Tibbets. I am the rector of the Holy Crusade Committee. We are here to spread the good word and bring the peace of the savior's teachings to this Sodom."

"That puts us in the same line of work, Sister. It's my job to bring peace too," Joe said.

"Hardly, Mr. Wiley. I bring the men of Mercury Wells the promise of an eternal life of bliss in the world invisible," she said with a smug tone. "You simply promise to send them there prematurely."

That reply trumped Joe's statement and he fished for a proper answer. They were arriving at a large tent staked down at the very edge of town. It glowed white from lanterns within against the blackness of the night beyond.

Sister Adeline handed off the girl to one of her flock as they filed into the tent. She muttered a word to one of the women who nodded before heading inside. Joe stood at the entrance to the tent with the woman in white.

"What about the girl?" he asked.

"We will enjoin her to become one of our ranks. She will be invited to seek forgiveness and follow us on the path to God's love," Sister Adeline said.

More than likely the girl would be back tomorrow selling her cunny to cowboys at fifty cents a throw, Joe thought but only nodded as though in approval of the sister's plans.

One of the women returned, stepping from the light within the tent to hand Sister Adeline Joe's coat before retreating. Adeline held the coat to him, allowing the collar to shift under her fingers, weighing it. Before he could take it from her, she had plucked the bible from the inside pocket. It was the same gilt-edged book he'd taken from the dead man all those years back. She looked at it in the muted light coming through the tent canvas.

"You read the word of God?" she said, an eyebrow raised.

"In quiet moments," he said, taking the coat from her hand.

"You wear a cross as well," she said, eyes to the tiny crucifix swinging on his watch chain as he slid the coat back on. She offered him the bible.

"A gift from the same man who gave me the book," he said, his hand lingering on her gloved fingers holding the book.

"A last gift?" she said, allowing him to maintain his grip on her hand, her thumb moving across the bullet hole in the book's cover.

"It was," he said.

"And has the book helped you make up your mind to follow the word of the Lord?" she said, opening her hand, allowing the book to slip from her grasp into his.

"I believe that the Lord is still making up His mind about me, Sister," Joe said, dropping the book back into his coat pocket and making his farewells.

As he walked from the moon glow of the tent toward the lantern lights of town, he heard the voices of women joined in song behind him.

See, the Conqueror mounts in triumph
See the King in royal state.
Riding on the clouds, His chariot
To His heavenly palace gate.
Hark! The choirs of angel voices
Joyful alleluias sing.
And the portals high are lifted
To receive their heavenly King.

Joe imagined he could divine Adeline's voice from among the others, sweet and melodic. As he walked past one den of sin followed by another, he touched his hand to his nose. There was the ghost of an aroma there of flowers and wine where he'd touched her gloved hand. An austere devotee dedicating her life to service to God Above who had just enough woman left in her to wear scent. Joe wondered what other mysteries might hide behind those opal-colored eyes.

He spun the chamber of his .44 to spill the empty rounds and reload the weapon as he walked back to the Paradise intent on his promise to return to the devil's work.

14

The drunks at the Paradise had grown in number, drawn there by the shootout. The curious and the idle come to flock about the pools of blood like desert birds around a water hole. The drovers stood over their fallen amigos, toasting their memory with shots of whiskey. Others stood viewing the two dead cowboys like they were museum exhibits or carnival curiosities. The recent gunplay was recounted again and again for newcomers, the lies compounding until the seconds-long fracas took on the stuff of legend.

"Phoo!" said the big drover, waving a hand before his face. "What's that stink?"

"I think it's Lem Dougal," another drover said, stopping by one of the corpses and sniffing the air. "Shat himself when that bassard gunned him."

"We're gonna see to that lawman. We're gonna settle him good. What he done weren't right. He needs to settle for poor Lem and… and…" said the big man, unable to recall the name of the other good friend growing cool in the crust of his own blood.

"We can settle up right now, cowboy," Joe Wiley said, making his way through the press to the bar.

The drovers swallowed their rage in a hurry. Except for the big man, the others couldn't meet the lawman's gaze. The big man kept working on his bleary stare. He meant it to sting but all it managed to do was make him look frog-eyed.

"Four men each, grab a wrist and ankle. Haul your friends over to Johansson's. Tell him to put it on my bill," Joe said, prodding one of the bodies with a toe of a boot. Johansson was the funeral director set up in a tent sitting well back of the main drag. Back where the stench of his customers, and the necessary chemicals to see them buried right, wouldn't trouble the citizenry. Joe covered the funeral expenses out of his "arrest" fund. Ten bucks for a pine box and a hole dug and even a word said over the departed. That left forty bucks pure profit from each "conviction."

The cowboys made their way out, toting their dead amigos. The big man followed, a glance back at Joe Wiley who ignored him to step to the bar.

"Who owns this pisshole?" Joe asked a bartender. The man blinked at him.

"You understand English?" Joe asked.

"This is my place, marshal."

Joe turned to see the roulette dealer stepping his way. A fussy little man in a green jacket trimmed in velvet at the collar and cuff over a silk vest. The man had a fixed squint that set his face in a permanently sour expression. Behind him stalked the shotgun man from the stool. Closer up, Joe could see the larger man was a half breed or maybe half Mex. Dark walnut skin and black eyes without a light in them. His face was that of a fighter—clubbed ears, crushed nose and the white hatchwork of old scars on his brows.

"Joe Wiley," Joe said without offering his hand. He took an instant dislike to the man in green and made no effort to hide it.

"I know who you are. You're the one keeps killing my customers. My name is T.J. Bratt. The Paradise is mine," the man said, making no struggle to conceal his own dislike. But he signaled the barman to set Joe up with a drink. The bartender slid a glass before Joe and tipped a bottle to it, filling it to the brim. Joe ignored it.

"I'll keep on coming in here until you get a rein on this place or until I've put a bullet in every last one of your patrons," Joe said, fixing Bratt with a hard look. "I've been in here three times since

I came to Mercury Wells. You need to get this place under heel, mister. I'll give you one day to hire yourself some kind of protection. Because every time I have to come through those doors someone's going to die. This time being the exception. For now. And that's not good for your custom."

The space under the tent had gone silent. The drinkers stopped their hoorahing and joshing to listen to the exchange with keen interest.

"Bear can keep the place settled down," Bratt said, jerking his head to the sullen shotgun man.

"Not so long as he sits his ass on that stool all day and night. Maybe your Bear needs some help," Joe said, turning to lean back with his elbows atop the bar plank.

"Like I said, marshal, the Paradise is my look-in," Bratt said, his squint narrowing, lips drawn tight over teeth that looked like kernels of dried corn.

"You can make my job harder or easier. You make this place troublesome enough and I'll shut you down." Joe flicked out a hand to slide the shot of whiskey away. It tumbled to the sand. He pushed off the bar and walked to the door, every eye on his back.

Out in the cool night air, Joe walked back along the boardwalk, now completed on the north side of the main drag all the way from the post office to The Double Eagle. The night was only started and looked to be a long one. The saloons, a half dozen, were full now with rowdies spilling out onto the street. A banjo playing Stephen Foster at The Patriot competed with a Mexican guitar at the Casa Blanco. The tent brothels would be just as packed later. Both enterprises were sources of fights, vandalism and deviltry. Drunken and horny cowboys, rail workers and drifters all liquored up and on the prod. He'd be walking this street until the sky turned rosy with morning light. For that he'd need coffee and he knew MacDougal would keep a pot steaming for him in the lobby of the Prairie. He'd head there and get a mug down him to hold him upright and eyes open.

Two riders cantering down the drag had to pull rein in front of The Busted Steer to avoid something laying out there in a wagon rut. One of the cowboys wheeled around to spit a stream of chaw at the shadowy shape before heading on his way. They rode away laughing.

Joe stepped down from the planks to walk out to where the humped shape lay unmoving in the dark roadway. It was a man lying prone. The stink of stale booze fought with the lemony smell of piss for supremacy. Joe put a boot sole on the man's ribs and gave a shove.

"You alive?"

The drunk snorted like a rutting pig in response.

"Do you know you're likely to get your head stove in by a wagon wheel laying here in the right of way?" Joe said, rocking the man once more. The only answer he received was a trumpeting fart.

"Come on, you damned souse," Joe said, lifting the man from the street by the collar and launching him stumbling for the boardwalk.

Joe stooped to snatch up the man's hat, a sombrero with a crushed crown. The marshal followed the drunk's weaving gait to where the man stopped, hugging a lantern pole as though afraid he'd slide off the planet and into the cosmos. Under the light of the guttering oil lamp, Joe could see the man's face. A broad mouth set in a shovel-flat face marked by a long vertical scar running from temple to jaw on the left side of his face. The bottom of the lobe of his left ear ended in a puckered scar. Lank black hair worn long to the collar. Most striking was the angle of the man's eyes, a pronounced slant over cheekbones set high, giving the man the look of a Mongol khan.

"Damn." Joe stared at him in a mix of disgust and building anger.

Coolie Taylor dropped to his knees and vomited over Joe's boots.

15

Coolie Taylor eventually came to with a volcanic hangover raging inside his skull. He looked about himself at a world that swirled in his vision as if seen through rippled glass. His mouth tasted like the bottom of a cow stall. He shook his head and blinked his eyes to clear them. Coolie then clasped his head in agony. A lightning bolt flashed through his skull to sear a point somewhere deep in his brain. He leaned forward on the wooden bunk, gripping the frame with his head between his knees.

"Christ! That was a mistake," Coolie said. His croak was followed by deep, agonized moans.

After a bit he finally looked up again and saw that he was in a cell in a modest looking but seemingly secure jail. Brick walls. A door of crossed iron bands. A slit window well above the reach of even a tall man set on the opposite wall and also covered in iron bands. Sunlight come in through the high window.

"Well shit," he muttered. His voice sounded to him like it was coming from the bottom of a well.

He ducked his head between his legs again. A door opened and boots clopped on the floor. Coolie looked up just in time to get a face full of chill water.

Joe Wiley dumped the entire bucket of ice-cold water onto Coolie and looked down on the now soaked man.

"GODDAMMIT! What the hell!" Coolie shouted and sputtered then winced as his own voice cut through his head like a saw blade.

"Good morning," Joe said.

"Damned if it is!" Coolie said in bitter disagreement.

Coolie looked up to give the lawman a piece of his mind and then saw it was Joe Wiley.

"I mighta known. Ol' Snakehand Wiley. The bible-toting bastard orphan gun hand."

"Well it shouldn't come as too much of a surprise since I summoned you here," Joe said.

Coolie screwed up his face in deep thought.

"Did ya? I guess I forgot," Collie said, and the light came on. "Oh yeah! Goldam if ya didn't!"

"I didn't wire you to come paint the town red."

"I thought I'd have a bracer or two after the train ride. Cut the dust."

"Then a shot or two turned to a dozen or two," Joe said, shaking his head.

"You know what I always say," Coolie said, looking up sheepish with eyes red as embers, "you ain't really drunk if you can lay on the floor without holding on."

"I need a deputy. Someone I can trust. Once you sober up, I'll let you out and swear you on. There is a lot of work to be done to cleanse this hellhole," Joe said, tossing the bucket in the corner and walking away from the cell. He swung the cell door shut behind him.

"Now just wait a goldamn minute! You let me out of here right now, Joe Wiley! I'm as sober as Sunday! And who sez I want to help you get killed and get killed myself in the process! You gotta lotta nerve, you do! Summon me here and treat me like this! Let me out!" Coolie said.

Joe, being used to Coolie's ways, ignored his ranting. He looked through the cage bars of the next cell to the two men he'd arrested from the Paradise on his first night in town.

"I'll have some hen fruit and beans sent over for breakfast. With some strong coffee to wash it down," Joe told them.

"When we getting out?" the uglier of the two asked. It was a close contest. The pair looked like what happens when first cousins marry.

"I am conferring with myself on the sentence. Just eat your breakfast and we'll see by the end of the day if you are properly chastised," Joe said.

"What the hell's that mean?" the other said.

"It means thank Jesus you didn't get what I gave your amigo," Joe said, making to walk away.

"What about me? Don't I get no breakfast?" Coolie asked.

"You'll just puke it up. And since you'll be the one cleaning it up…" Joe said.

Coolie closed his yap and stewed in silence as he lay dripping on the soaked bunk.

Joe left the jailhouse and walked over to a hash house. It was a simple place serving cheap, filling food to those hungry and in a hurry. No tablecloths here. No tables either. Men sat on benches eating from tin plates balanced on their knees. The man running it was a towering figure with a handlebar mustache and strands of hair pomaded across his scalp.

"I need two orders of eggs and beans and some coffee to be run over to my prisoners at the jailhouse," Joe said and dropped a dollar on the counter with a silvery plink.

"Will do, marshal," the roughhouse cook said. "Anything for yourself?"

"No thanks. I'll grab something later." Joe nodded and walked from the tent and almost smack dab into Mayor Tuchman.

"Marshal, I need a word or two with you," His Honor said.

"Well spit them out," Joe said. He nodded at Ned Merriweather and Bob Miller who tagged along with His Honor.

"The two men you gunned down last night were employees of the Twisted Tree Ranch. Big Cal Randall isn't going to like that. He's ramrod for the Tree."

"Oh my, no," Merriweather echoed.

"Well, that's tough for Big Cal," Joe said. "You are paying me to settle this town down to a purr. I can't do that by pussyfooting around. I'll only spill as much blood as I need to. So, tell Randall to let his men know to behave themselves and they'll be able to keep working for him. Otherwise…"

"Otherwise, what?" the mayor said.

"I start posting cowboys out of town. That means barring them. And a deadline either side of town where they surrender their arms. Meaning I'd need more deputies than stipulated in our contract," Joe said.

"The city would pay for them, I suppose?" Merriweather put in.

"Or let me handle this the way I see fit. Arrests where possible and convictions where necessary."

The mayor and banker understood that by "convictions" their new marshal meant another unmarked grave in the growing cemetery just outside of town.

Merriweather prodded the mayor with an elbow. The mayor sighed, irritated, and cut his eyes at the banker.

"I'm handling this, Ned."

Merriweather cleared his throat and stepped away down the plank-way.

The mayor looked back at Joe beseechingly, wet eyes glimmering.

"Marshal, Mercury Wells counts on the cowboys and hands that work on that spread. If this town is to thrive, we need their money for our businesses. It's not all about the railroad."

Joe nodded.

"I get that. I do. But this town also needs order to survive. Once the cowboys understand that this town isn't wide open to their hellraising anymore, they'll settle down. You need to pick a side, Mr. Mayor," Joe said.

Without a word of farewell, Joe brushed aside the mayor and eyeballed Bob Miller for a moment. The county constable was coming up the walk. He stepped aside but not without a disapproving glance at the new marshal. Joe fixed him with a look before heading across the street to the Texas and New Orleans telegraph office. The three men watched his departure with displeasure.

"He told me to pick a side," Mayor Tuchman said.

"It's more complicated than that," the reedy little banker said.

"There might come a time to end his contract, Mr. Mayor," Bob Miller said, thumbs hooked in his gun belt.

Joe stepped into the modest shack that served as the telegraph office by the station house. Tending to things was a boy not much older than he was when Ben Temple found him fighting for scraps in the street. A towheaded, small-framed boy who seemed to Joe to be naturally agreeable.

"Anything for me, son?" Joe Wiley asked.

"Yes, sir, it just come in a bit ago. I was gonna run it down to you when I got a chance." The young man eagerly handed Joe the telegram. The printing on the Western Mail paper was neatly penciled in a schoolboy hand. The boy stared at the new marshal with not a little bit of hero worship in his young eyes. Word got around fast it seemed. The new lawman was a genuine gunhand.

"Much obliged." Joe nodded.

Joe read the message and a wry smile grew across his face. He crushed the paper and tossed it to the floor, tousled the youth's hair and departed the office with an easier gait than he used when entering.

The boy bent down and retrieved the ball of paper and opened it back up. He wrapped his wire spectacles around his ears. He reread the message that had been sent to the marshal. He looked up in wonder.

"Who are the Dugans?" he asked no one in particular.

16

That evening, Joe Wiley made his way to the Majestic. Shorty Little certainly wasn't wrong about the place. By a sizeable margin it was the largest saloon and game house in Mercury Wells. The place certainly looked more welcoming and classier than did the Paradise or any other, similar places in town. Joe could hear the pipe organ music long before he entered. The orchestral thunder of it made a hum in the wood planks of the boardwalk. He expected Ben Temple was pleased with it.

Inside, a monumental mahogany bar ran the length of the barroom from one side to the other then back again. The customers included railroad construction workers, cowboys, townspeople, Chinese and Mexicans, drug fiends, thieves, and wantons. There was gambling, of course. Faro, roulette, dice and poker. An enormously fat woman in layers of gingham twirled a parasol where she stood and sang on a raised stage not much bigger than one of the cells back at the jail. Her accompaniment was provided by an extravagant Mason and Hamlin four octave organ in a rosewood cabinet. Those afflicted from the lingering loneliness of riding the range or leveling rail gradings could, for a small remuneration, find solace in the cribs upstairs. And, of course, one could spend money on drink.

Joe was pleased to note that the place was professionally managed. He spied four rough looking men seated on tall stools and armed with sawed-off pick handles. One had a fancy nickel-plated revolver in a holster slung under his left arm in a leather rig. One would need to take a second thought to mix with them.

Ben was seated at a corner table, his back to a wall. The perfect place for a blind man to hold court. He wasn't alone either. A young whore was seated close to him, all smiles as Ben regaled her with some story or other. Who knew how much of it was bullshit or all too true. The man was a notorious liar. Especially to women. It was getting so the line between lie, legend and fact were all blurred in Ben's imagination. She hung on his every word regardless. Joe pulled back one of the heavy oaken chairs and took a seat.

"Well, I see you didn't take long settling in. And finding yourself a friend," Joe said.

"Some of us are better at making friends. And some of us are better at making enemies," Ben said through a grin. A cigar stuck out of one side of his mouth, a thin cheroot with a tip of gray ash. "This is Clara Belle. She is keeping me company, as we enjoy the excellent music and ambiance of this fine establishment. Clara Belle, this is Joe Wiley. My oldest acquaintance."

Clara Belle extended a gloved hand. Joe took it and gave it a cautious near peck, not actually touching the cloth with his lips. The glove smelled of stale tobacco and rancid *parfum*. The whore was young but not what one would call pretty. She had the watery eyes and sallow skin of an opium user. But then, to Ben, she could appear as Helen of Troy and Cleopatra rolled into one. In his world of perpetual night he knew only the limits of his imagination.

"I am very pleased to meet you, Mr. Wiley," Clara Belle said, her other hand to her mouth, fingers hiding teeth stained brown from smoking the black tar.

"The treat is all mine," Joe said, his smile fixed and only going so far as the corners of his mouth. His eyes remained hooded in shadow under his hat, which he only removed indoors when in the presence of a lady. Joe felt the need for a woman as much as any man but did not share Ben's taste for whores. He found them unappealing and sad. So many of them succumbed to consumption and worse in their pitifully brief careers. As a lawman, he'd found too many of these so-called soiled doves lying dead and discarded in alleyways and muddy streets, cast aside like a worn saddle blanket or an empty jug.

"Clara Belle can read and has generously agreed to visit me in my room to read to me of an evening," Ben said.

"Good to hear. Takes some of the load off of me. I frankly find Charles Dickens tedious," Joe said.

"Joseph prefers Dumas. But then he has always been an incurable romantic." Ben smiled easy, blind eyes crinkled in amusement at his friend. The whore giggled behind splayed fingers.

At that moment a dark-haired man of slender build, with a neatly trimmed mustache and clad in fine clothes, came to the table and greeted the new arrival.

"*Bonjour!* Welcome to Mercury Wells and especially welcome to The Majestic, Marshal Wiley. I am Marcelle DeGeaux, the owner. I would be honored to serve you your favorite drink *sans frais pour vous, bien sûr*. On the house, of course."

"Well, that would be kind of you. Thanks, Mr. DeGeaux. Just a good beer would go down nicely," Joe said and took DeGeaux's offered hand. Soft hands. They hadn't seen much work. The hands of a man used to paying others to do for him.

DeGeaux snapped his fingers at a server and instructed him to fetch a beer.

"We are very happy to have you in our humble town. I want to assure you that I run a clean house from the tables to my ladies," DeGeaux said. "We need law and order to grow into what our dreams envision. And having a strong lawman is *très bien*. It is good business, *non*?"

"Well I'm happy to hear that, Mr. DeGeaux. And I aim to make that happen. So DeGeaux, eh? That's French. Where you hail from?" Joe asked.

"France itself, *monsieur*. I was in the French Foreign Legion. I was at the Battle of Camarón under Emperor Maximillian. I made my way from Mexico here to Texas to build a better life," DeGeaux said.

"That was one hell of a skirmish down Mexico way I've heard. Lucky you got out alive," Joe said. "But it looks like you are succeeding in that new life of yours. And I appreciate you're making the effort to keep a lid on this place." His beer arrived. He nodded at the nearest stool man, the one with the shiny revolver.

"But of course. Enjoy yourselves and come back and come often. *Bonsoir!*" DeGeaux said excusing himself from the table. Joe lifted his mug at the man's departure.

"French army my dead eyes. I've already got word that he is more likely just a coon-ass pimp up from New Orleans putting a luster on himself," Ben said and made a dismissive noise. "And double bullshit he was at Camarón. Not a single frog-gigger walked away from that tussle."

Clara Belle stifled another giggle.

"As long as he keeps his nose clean and this place away from trouble I don't care where he says he came from," Joe said and drained his mug.

Ben nodded. "Fair enough I reckon. A man's past don't matter in this country."

"Only what he makes of himself," Joe said, nodding.

"And women?" Clara said, eyes lifting to study the new marshal, lingering on the silver crucifix on its chain.

"Women are like flowers," Ben said, fingers playing up her thigh. "They are as God made them, a wondrous, unchanging creation and source of delight."

The whore let out a whooping laugh at that, slapping at the blind man's exploring hand but only gently.

"Enjoy the rest of your evening. I'll see you back at the Prairie later," Joe said, rising.

Joe stepped from the heat and noise of the Majestic into the cool night air. As he moved out into the street, he became aware of a group of cowboys giving him the stink eye. Beyond returning their baleful stares with a cold mask of indifference, he ignored them and continued on his way.

As Ben Temple had been known to say: "Don't kick a dog to see if he'll bite. Better to assume that he'll turn on you given the chance."

17

Joe Wiley stood on the rough boards at the station house, his eyes closed, his face raised to the afternoon sun. He pushed back the brim of his hat to feel the warmth on his cheeks. The clink of spurs and creak of leather approached from behind him. The thumb of his left hand remained tucked behind his gun belt.

A voice spoke from the boards at his back. "You recall meeting me at this very spot a few days back?"

Joe turned to find Homer Gibbs standing in the sun before a shorter man with a sour expression screwed on his face. The other man wore a short-barreled Smith in a pocket holster slung before his crotch. Another cowboy in fringed chaps of frayed leather. A stubby man with a barrel chest and a face that looked like it had seen a lot of hard miles. Two more drovers leaned against the station house wall in the shade of an awning, hands resting on gun belts. One of them was from the welcoming party Gibbs hosted here a few days before. His Sharps leaned against the wall beside him.

"Gibbs. Ramrod and foreman of the Three Rivers, right?" Joe said easy.

"That's right. This here is Big Cal Randall, boss of the Twisted Tree," Homer said, his face impassive, eyes hard.

Joe clamped his lips together to prevent a laugh from escaping. This squirt was the "Big" Cal the mayor was going on about? He swallowed the smile but couldn't prevent the corners of his mouth turning up. The lemon-sucker sensed it. His nose wrinkled. His eyes turned to twin gun sights.

"You had no call gunnin' down Rufus and Charlie," Cal Randall said, voice as bitter as his face.

"Where'd this happen again?" Joe said.

"Down the Paradise. You did them in cold blood."

"You weren't there, mister. You don't know what call I may or may not have had to act as I did." Joe turned from the man at the far-off squeal of a steam whistle. A white column of smoke was rising from the north stretch of track. The train he'd been waiting on since morning was coming along.

"The fellas 'spect to come into town and burr the edge off some. They work and pay their money to have fun is all," the little man said through his teeth.

"Pulling a gun on me ain't my idea of fun. Mister," Joe said, his tone darkening.

The little man stepped closer, his mouth working to speak again.

"I ain't engaging in an argument with you," Joe said. "The law is the law, and the law is what I say. Your drovers are free to come to this town and poke all the cunny they can afford to poke. But I don't hold with terrorizing whores. Bad enough those girls got to lay with those busters. They don't need to tolerate some bastard cutting at them. That's where I intercede."

Big Cal blinked, trying to decide what "intercede" might mean.

"Well," Big Cal said after a long pause, "you watch your back else someone inner-seeds *you* one dark night."

Joe stepped to within inches of the smaller man, his fingertips drummed a tattoo on the leather near his slant-mounted .36. Big Cal had to crane his neck back to meet the marshal's gaze. He looked like a lizard on a rock.

"I'll take that as a caution, cowboy," Joe said low for only the other man to hear. "Because if I ever suspected, even for one blessed second, that those words were any kind of threat I'd make you pull that piece you wear where your cock should be."

The smaller man paled, swallowed hard, and backed well away before turning for the steps down from the platform.

"Do we have business, friend?" Joe said, turning to Homer Gibbs who was watching the lawman with a cool appraisal.

"Mr. Nostrand was wondering when you might be releasing those two Three Rivers men you're holding."

"In the morning. Does that suit Mr. Nostrand?" Joe said, the fury fading from his voice. The locomotive had reached the edge of the platform and was hissing and banging to a stop along the boards.

"The boss paid you a fat bonus for turning up here in Mercury Wells. He's as interested as you in seeing this town calmed down to a roar. He ain't at all pleased you killed one man of his and jailed two more," Gibbs said.

"That sack of eagles supposed to buy your boys some slack with me?" Joe said.

"Maybe a bit of consideration," Gibbs said.

"Then maybe you need to take it back to your boss," Joe said. "Maybe he could use it to buy himself another marshal."

"You need to recall that you're only one man, Wiley. You have a reputation, that's sure. But that only carries you till you have to prove it," Gibbs said, an edge to his words. His two amigos pushed off the wall of the station house and stepped into the sunlight, hands loose at their sides.

"And will I have to prove it?" Joe said, corner of his mouth curling. His fingers drummed again on his leather.

"We ain't drunk, marshal," Gibbs said, the edge turning razor sharp. His hand dropped to brush the Colt nestled snug in its Mexican rig.

Joe's smile froze on his face. His back to the slowing train. A cloud of expelled steam cut around him in a swirling tide. He looked like nothing less than a vengeful angel surrounded by the billowing clouds of the hereafter. His eyes weighed the three men as they locked on him, hands drifting with minds of their own for the draw.

"Damn me all to hell and back again!" boomed a voice behind Joe.

Two men emerged from the falling mist of engine steam followed by a porter lumbering with a trunk in his arms. Both men wore woolen suits over boiled shirts and paper collars. Their heads were topped with bowlers, waxed mustaches perched on their upper lips. They moved with the assured authority of men who feared nothing, cocks of the walk and kings of the jungle. That impression was enforced by the revolvers that hung from their hips and, especially, by the double barrel ten-gauge coach guns cradled in the crooks of their right arms.

"Boys, I'd like you to meet Homer Gibbs, ramrod and foreman of the Three Rivers ranch," Joe said, beaming at the newcomers. "I failed to catch the name of his two companions."

The two arrivals blinked at Joe. The porter grunted under the weight of the trunk. Joe turned to complete the introductions but Gibbs and his drovers, their backs to him, were moving away off the platform for town.

"Sorry, boys. I suppose they had a previous engagement," Joe said and stuck out a hand to the two men.

"You're already stirring the shit," Len Dugan said, smiling as he took Joe's hand in a crushing grip.

"And expectin' us to join hands and jump in it with him," Seth Dugan said, less pleased than his brother with his first impression of Mercury Wells.

18

"Ain't we been here before?" Seth said, his disdain deepening as they followed Joe across to the jailhouse, the porter huffing behind them under the weight of the trunk.

"It does look like every other shithole cowtown we've been to, brother," Len agreed.

"It is the same as Waring Station and Riverford," Joe assured them. "And it'll pay out like they did."

Joe held up a hand to stop a water wagon's progress down the main drag. The wagon was pulled by two dray horses to spray water over the street to damp down the summer dust. They crossed before it to the boardwalk.

"What's the pay, Joe?" Len asked.

"You'll be working off a commission out of my end. Twenty bucks for each arrest."

"And how much for each dead lawbreaker?" Seth asked.

"Ten bucks per conviction. Again, paid by me. I don't want to encourage you boys to over exuberance."

Len informed Seth that this meant that Joe wanted the gunfights held to a minimum.

When they reached the jailhouse, they found Ben Temple playing chess with Coolie Taylor through the bars of Coolie's cell.

"How you know he's not cheating you, blind man?" Seth said by way of announcing his arrival.

"I have numbered the spaces on the board, you Finnian turd," Ben said without turning from the game. "My opponent tells me which space his piece occupies and therefore I can keep the status of the game locked away in my unassailable mind."

"I tried cheating. He caught me," Coolie grumped, arm through the bars, fingertips hovering over the crown atop his queen.

"You remember the Dugan brothers," Joe said.

"I remember I busted one of their noses over a horse trade in Clabber Mills," Coolie said, removing his fingers from the queen to pluck up his remaining knight.

"That was me and it was Antelope up in the territories." Len grinned.

"How's Coolie doing, Ben?" Joe asked.

"He plays the game of kings like a slow child," Ben said.

"I meant as pertains to sobriety and you damn well know I did."

"Oh, he's sober enough. Still can't keep down hot food though. Pukes it up or shits it out," Ben said, an ear cocked to hear the tap of the errant knight dropping to the board surface.

"Couple more days then," Joe said.

"That was a move," Ben said, peeved. "Sing out the number, Coolie."

"I ain't decided and my hand's still on it, son of a bitch," Coolie hissed.

"I'll take you boys to the hotel," Joe said, turning to the Dugans.

"We'll be fine stayin' right here," Len said.

"We prefer brick walls around us when working for you, Wiley," Seth added, frowning.

The porter lowered the trunk to the floor, heaving a grateful sigh of relief. Two bits in his sweating palm, he retired.

"Well then, I'll ask our other guests to vacate your bunks early," Joe said, snatching a ring of keys from a hook and unlocking the cell containing the pair of Three Rivers cowboys. The pair stepped from the cell, eyes darting from the marshal to the two new strangers.

"Take a good look at these two. You see either or both of them back in town before Saturday you feel free to blow their heads off," Joe said, patting one of the men on the back like a treasured friend. The Dugans eyed the drovers. Twenty bucks on the hoof. Joe turned to the cowboys.

"Tell your foreman I'm not fining you this time. But next time it's a dollar a day," Joe said, shooing them before him to the street door. He tossed their gun belts, ammunition loops empty, to the boardwalk behind them.

"Buy yourself some bullets on the way out of town. I confiscated your lead," Joe said before shutting the jailhouse door on them.

"So, what's this town like? Really?" Len Dugan asked, helping himself to a mug of coffee.

"Fat," Joe said with a grin. "I figure we have six months to a year here to bring peace to this shithole. There's money to be made, boys. So long as you don't mind some blood on your sleeve."

"Long as I don't have to do my own laundry," Seth Dugan said with a face of stone. The others stared at him. Even Ben Temple turned to fix his unseeing gaze on the Irishman.

"I do believe your brother made a joke," Joe said.

"I wouldn't bet on that," Len said with a shake of his head.

"And I wouldn't take that bet," Ben said.

They snorted laughter. All but Seth who did not mean his remark as a joke and Coolie who found that laughter only brought on further bouts of the squirts.

19

The Mayor of Mercury Wells took another sip of blended rye. He knew it would only stoke the fire in his belly. But what was a man to do? Not for the first time he envied the wretches lying insensate down in the tents run by the Chinese. A pipe of the black smoke might be just what was called for given the recent developments in town.

He crumpled the yellow paper of the most recent telegram and tossed it across the upstairs drawing room of the Majestic. He kicked at the little Negro whore who was sharing the settee with him. She'd been rubbing his bare feet and shrank from his sudden lashing out.

"Something troubling come down the wire, Geoffrey?" Marcelle DeGeaux said from a flocked velvet chair behind a desk of carved black mahogany.

"Nothing but trouble comes down the wire from as far as Chicago," Tuchman said and shifted on the settee. His hand reached out to pat the little hand of the black girl. He tapped the flat of his hand to the cushion beside him. She joined him on the settee, smiling with shy eyes.

"Our masters are not pleased?" DeGeaux said with maddening calmness. He'd told the mayor that it was his natural *sang froid*. Tuchman thought the pimp was as coldhearted as a river snake.

"They are not. They tasked me with finding a lawman. I took Nostrand's suggestion and hired this Wiley fellow," Tuchman said as he idly played with one of the young whore's teats.

"This is trouble?"

"It damn sure is. The man's doing his job a sight too enthusiastically. And now he's brought these Dugans to town."

"I have heard of them."

"You damned sure have, Marcelle!" The mayor snorted, startling the whore with a sharp squeeze. "They're a pair of bloody-handed murderers! They settled that range war up in Wyoming. They're *still* finding dead nesters up there. And that massacre in Oklahoma. They're not lawmen. They're exterminating sons of bitches."

"I do not see what it matters. We want law. We have law." DeGeaux shrugged.

"We might end up with more law than we want. There are long term plans for this town that go beyond cow shit and water for steam. A lot of money has been poured into this godforsaken corner of Texas. And the men who do the pouring expect a return on their investment."

"You are a man who worries. It is not good to worry. Life is to be enjoyed moment to moment."

"I wish I shared your damned Gallic sense of the trivial."

"I see that you are inconsolable. And so, I shall leave you to the attentions of little Nubia," DeGeaux said, standing from his chair. After taking a last draught of brandy from a tumbler, he stepped from the room, securing the door behind him.

"Well, what shall we do then, my dear?" the mayor said, turning from the door to the impish smile of the child now crawling over the cushions into his lap.

20

The town's headlong rush to debauchery slowed as sunrise approached. The oil lamps were extinguished. The saloons shuttered. The star-shot sky above was giving way to a salmon-colored dawn. Joe Wiley made his last pass along the main drag, kicking drunks awake. Telling them if they didn't have a place to stay then at least get out of sight before the stores opened for business.

The night before was quieter than most. Most of the drovers were spread out all over the hills to the north and south gathering steers for shipment. A few bunkhouse creepers made it into town. There were some fights and indiscriminate gunfire. Only four arrests and no one was convicted. No work for the gravedigger.

The Dugans joined Joe as he walked back toward the jail. Coolie Taylor sat in a chair on the boardwalk, tipped back and sipping coffee from a mug. The Dugans made their way inside to their bunks in the spare cell. The main cell was loaded with four drovers pitched out of the Majestic for fighting. They'd tried to return inside, prompting a battle on the boardwalk with the Frenchman's toughs. The hardest part of the arrest for the Dugans was loading the unconscious cowboys onto a cart and rolling them down to the jailhouse.

"Ben let you out?" Joe said.

"Kept steak and beans and a hunk of pie down all night." Coolie beamed.

"You can keep an eye on things till noon then?" Joe said.

"Me and John Henry," Coolie said, patting the brass Henry rifle that rested across his knees.

"Then I'm going to lay my head down a few hours," Joe said, walking away along the plank walk.

"Go easy, amigo," Coolie said, drawing a mouthful of honey-sweetened coffee thick enough to float a horseshoe.

At the Grand Prairie, Joe listened at Ben Temple's door and heard nothing. The man was sleeping it off elsewhere or catting around with one of the girls at the Majestic. Joe entered his own dark room. A white shape that hadn't been there when he left lay in the gloom. Years of instinct had him out of the bar of light from the hallway and into the darkness by the door, the .44 drawn and cocked in his hand.

The white shape made no moves. His eyes adjusted to the gloom. It was something draped over a chair, folds dropping to the floor. His eyes swept the room as did the long barrel of the revolver. He stepped to the chair. The cloth was cool between his fingers. Lace trim crinkled as he lifted it from the chair.

A tinkle of feminine laughter in the dark.

Joe stepped to the bed to see the covers shift over a slim form moving there. A fan of corn silk hair spread across the pillows. Slender fingers clutched the sheet drawn up to her chin.

"Sister Adeline Tibbets?"

She laughed again. More heartily this time.

"Is this any way for a nun to act?" Joe said, smiling.

"I'm not a nun, you idiot," she said.

"You left a whole lot of clothes over there, Sister."

"Uh huh."

"What have you left to cover yourself?"

"Only what God gave me," she said lifting her chin, her eyes gone smoky in the dark.

Joe lifted the sheet to see the bounty of the Lord.

They ate a very late breakfast together in the cozy dining room of the Grand Prairie. Hamish MacDougal waited on them himself, bringing plates of bacon, biscuits and an omelet of peppers and scallions. If the Scotsman noticed that Sister Adeline came down the stairs moments before the marshal, he was pretending he hadn't seen a thing.

"Another fine, skillet-hot, dust-devil summer day in Texas," Joe said in an attempt to start a civilized conversation.

They talked of the weather a bit. At the same time their eyes created an entirely different discourse. Hamish repaired to the kitchen for fresh cream and Adeline took the opportunity to reach across the table to steal a squeeze of Joe's arm. Her fingers leapt back upon Hamish's return. His eyes darted between them and his cheeks reddened before retreating to the front desk in the lobby.

When they were alone again, she said, "I might mistake you for a man of God."

His fingers went unconsciously to the crucifix dangling from his watch chain.

"I've read the book. Mostly for the stories." He shrugged, lifting a knife to slather butter on a biscuit.

"And the preacher's coat and the cross?"

"Took them both off a dead man a long time back. The Jesus anyway. Replaced the coat a time or two. I like the cut of it."

"Did you kill the man? Is that hole in the bible of your making?" she asked, a matter of curiosity only.

"No. Not me. I don't think so anyway. That night was a long time back, like I said."

"Have you embraced the God of love?"

He glanced up at her, searching her face for a hint of double meaning. Her face was a mask of wide-eyed innocence. He noted a turn at the corner of her lips and thought for a hot second or two about bundling her back upstairs to his bed.

"I have not experienced any such God of love or peace or anything like it."

"You need to seek His love. It's there for all of us," she said.

"Is that what you were doing blowing into the Paradise swinging an axe handle?" he said, amused at her widening eyes. The spray of freckles across her nose colored.

"That girl was–"

"That girl was going to die after those coyotes had gone at her right there on that bar," Joe said. "And all the hymns and sermons in the world weren't going to alter that one speck. You may love Jesus, Sister, but you came on with the god of the Hebrews in your heart."

"Is that your god, marshal?"

"I'm not a Jew if that's what you mean. But I have seen the wrath of God. I was a sinner, me and Ben Temple both, and we ran with sinners. And I saw our company struck down by God's wrath one by each until only Ben and I were left."

"Don't you see? You were spared by God's love," she said, reaching out touch his hand.

"We were spared to be witnesses," Joe said, his voice turning brittle. "Don't make any mistakes, Addy. Me and Ben were every bit as bad as the bastards we rode with. We were every bit as deserving of the Lord's scorn as the men I buried."

"But you took the cross, you took the book," she said, withdrawing her hand.

"To remind me. So, I'd never forget. So, I'd never backslide and take the easy way of stealing and killing. To make my trade standing against men like the man I once was," he said, placing his fork on his plate, the meal untouched but for a bite of biscuit.

"And how does it remind you?"

"It makes me recall that if God loves anything it's order. He spared me to bring back the balance where things have gone a'kilter.

He brought my life back to balance and I work every day and every night to keep the scales level. You singing and preaching and hectoring drunks and whores has a place out here, I suppose. But it ain't never going to take hold without men like me grading the way."

She lowered her eyes, nodding. He pushed his chair back from the table and rose.

"Now, you enjoy this fine breakfast, Sister. I have to see to the jailhouse and make sure my hungover, lazybutt deputies are up and moving." He restored his hat to his head and tipped the brow.

Sister Adeline turned in her chair after he'd left the dining room. Through the windows of the front windows, she could see Joe Wiley step out under the yellow sky, the bottle glass creating multiple images of him before he passed out of sight.

" 'And it will consume her citadels amid war cries on the day of battle, and a storm on the day of tempest,' " she said to herself.

"Excuse me, ma'am?" Hamish said from the doorway. "Ye say a storm is coming?"

"It is, Mr. MacDougal," she said, turning to him with a wan smile. "And the deluge will touch us all."

21

Cowboys from the Three Rivers whooped and swung coiled lariats to urge a thousand-head herd down the main drag to the stockyard where they expertly manipulated the cattle into the holding pens. They were eager to be done with the work and eager to be drowning their sorrows with beer and sharing them with some soft company. A mile or more of cattle strung out all the way to the blue hills leaving a plume of yellow dust hanging in the sky above.

The work that morning was dirty, noisy and tiring. Even for Joe Wiley and his deputies who kept the street clear of traffic as the beeves moved by at a trot. The town turned out to watch the parade go by with hollers and waves. The town fathers stood on the plank walk before the post office, smoking cigars and watching the passage of money on the hoof. All were covered in trail dust as surely as if they'd rolled in the stuff.

Behind the last steer, the water wagon trundled along to damp the dust down with spray. The citizens retreated into their homes and businesses, slapping grit from their clothes with their hats. The saloons opened in anticipation of the rush of cowboys sure to come once the beeves were home and penned.

Joe sent the Dugans and Coolie to breakfast and took a seat in a kitchen chair he set on the walk before the jailhouse.

A horse and buggy rolled up the street, splashing through the new mud created by the water wagon. It was a fine rig to look at. Black lacquered with tall wheels and bright yellow spokes. It was decorated

with gilt scroll work and the rear compartment was covered with a black canopy of cloth that shimmered like satin in the sun. The twin team of horses pulling it were just as black and just as shiny. They gamboled along like show horses rather than nags. A stern-faced Indo-Mexican held the traps. Joe noted a coach gun leaning against the Mex's far leg. He'd never seen this rig or the driver in town before.

The brougham pulled to a stop before the jailhouse, the Mex clucking at the reins. A man stepped from the shade of the canopy to the street. A tall man in an eastern dude suit of tweed topped by the biggest Stetson hat Joe had ever seen. Tall white crown with a silver ring and a brim near round about as a Mexican sombrero. The man looked at a blob of mud on the toe of one boot with disdain.

"Take care of the team and buggy and meet me at the Grand Prairie, Diego," the man said, stepping to the boardwalk. He was maybe in his forties or a fit man in his fifties. A hint of paunch behind his vest.

"*Sí*," the driver answered in a low baritone before flicking the reins to move away.

"Can I assume that you're Marshal Wiley? I'm Hector Nostrand," the stranger in the big Stetson said and offered a hand.

"You may assume so. Pleased to finally meet the big man. Thought for a time you might be one of those absentee owners," Joe said, standing to take Nostrand's hand. The grip was firm for a man with hands as soft as the easterner's.

"No, marshal. I'm not, at heart, a trusting man. I like to see where my money is being made as well as where it's being spent." Nostrand held his grip until he'd said his peace then released Joe's hand. He was a man used to being heard out.

"I thought it was past time we met," Joe said. "I see your boys have brought in a big herd, and I imagine a big hankering for some fun and frolic. And possible trouble."

"They're hard-working men, marshal. I find the harder a man works the harder he needs to play," Nostrand said.

"I get that." Joe nodded. "Done it a time or two myself. But it's how hard they play that brings them across my trail."

"Can't you take it a bit easy with my boys? They don't mean any harm."

"They may not mean harm, but some have caused it. No sir. I can't go easier on them then I do. They know where the line is. As long as I wear this badge that's where the line stays."

"I understand that. I'll offer a compromise," Nostrand said. "I won't pay my boys until after the cattle cars are loaded tomorrow."

"I appreciate the cooperation. You keep them down to the stockyard tonight. Give them a night to settle," Joe said.

"Think nothing of it. I'm a citizen of Mercury Wells myself. I have vested interests in this town and mean to see it do well. Have a good day, Marshall. You can find me at the Grand Prairie if you have need of me." Nostrand made his way down the wooden walkway toward the hotel.

Joe watched as the rancher departed, noticing for the first time that the man wore no firearm. None that was visible in any case.

Despite the fact they weren't paid yet, a bunch of cowboys were determined to have some fun and made their way into Mercury Wells. Tired of camping rough in the stockyard, and with just enough coins in their pokes to get drunk, they headed for the cheapest drinks in town. The Paradise.

As luck, or the lack of it, would have it, some Irishmen working for Southwest General Railroad were in town as well. And both groups wound up in T.J. Bratt's bucket of blood.

Details were hazy afterwards, but most could agree it started when a cowboy tried to share a navvy's bottle uninvited. The Irishman objected. Imprecations and oaths. Accusations of "shite-eating Yankee" and "pig-eyed Mick" flew wild. More bitter words were exchanged and then fists, bottles and chair legs. The barmen pulled pick handles, not to intercede in the riot but to protect the liquor stores behind the bar. T.J. Bratt himself, content to let the fight play out, retreated behind his roulette table. Bear, his bodyman, covered the heaving mob of combatants with his double barrel.

The Dugans arrived at a run. Seth attempted his own brand of reason by discharging both barrels of his shotgun through the canvas ceiling. The cowboys and rail men failed to notice. The fight went on without a second's pause. Len waded into the melee swinging his shotgun like a club. His brother followed. The two brothers cut a swath through the center of the fight, ending the dustup with brutal expediency. Men fell to the left and right. A drover held an arm with a snapped bone bulging against the fabric of his shirt. A son of Erin knelt on the sawdust floor spitting bloody teeth into his hand. More men dropped and remained where they fell. A cowboy howled and rolled on the floor, clutching a knee shattered by the brass butt of Len's shotgun.

Eventually a craggy faced cowboy jerked a revolver and invited his compatriots to join along.

"Blow these bastards back to hell!" he shouted, gun hand wavering at the Dugans.

Two of his fellow trail riders, equally as drunk, followed his lead.

Len's double barrel opened up while Seth reloaded his own.

The cowboys were thrown back as though by a massive scythe. Two lay knocked cold and bleeding out. A third sat on his ass for a moment looking stunned, raising a fingerless hand that had held a Colt a moment before. He collapsed backward and lay still, his chest peppered through with buck shot.

Even the Irish sobered up at the sight of this demonstration of the rule of law as it existed in Mercury Wells.

"Surrender your guns!" Len roared as he broke the shotgun open, two smoking cartridges flying.

"You heard my brother! On the floor. Right this minute!" Seth boomed, swinging his own shotgun around the circle of men while his sibling reloaded.

Cowboys dropped an assortment of pistols to the sand and sawdust. The Irish produced their own pistols hidden on their persons including a pepperbox derringer that looked like it would be as much a danger to the shooter as to any intended victim.

"Pick them up, boy!" Len said to a barman who stooped and gathered the surrendered weapons into a hammock made from his apron front.

"We ain't arresting anyone tonight so long as you make your way back to where you belong," Seth said and motioned to the tent opening with his shotgun. The cowboys, navvies and other patrons shuffled out; eyes lowered.

"This place is closed until otherwise determined by Marshal Wiley," Seth said to T.J. Bratt who only shrugged and nodded.

"Call your hound off," Len rumbled, eyes on Bear who stood with his own shotgun trained on the room.

"Call it a night, Bear," Bratt said in a voice of patience one might take with a child. The big man lowered the barrels, eyes still locked on Len Dugan.

"Follow us, boy. We're taking that iron down to the jail for safekeeping," Seth said and waved the barkeep forward. The barkeep looked to T.J. Bratt who nodded, giving him pardon to do as the deputy requested. The man departed the Paradise, bent double with the weight of an apron front loaded with pistols.

22

Daylight brought no lasting peace to either Mercury Wells in general or the Paradise in particular. Though this time it wasn't drunken drovers or Irishmen at the heart of the trouble.

Adeline Tibbets led the sisters of her congregation in a revival meeting of sorts on the street outside the Paradise. She was using the boardwalk in front of the pit of degradation as her pulpit. Her testimony was delivered with fire and conviction and a crowd soon joined the sisters to listen—for the entertainment and diversion if not enlightenment. A few men, still drunk from the night before, made to jeer at her until quieted by hard glances from the sisters. The even harder pick handles in their fists went a long way to improve the manners of the hecklers.

"Good liquor, clean women and fair tables," she pronounced, an accusing finger stabbing at the words on the shingle hung over the tent opening.

"What *good* is liquor for but to steal a man's senses and cause him to greater sin? How *clean* is a woman who will sell her charms to any man with the price? How *fair* is a game that always sends a man away penniless?

"These are *lies*, sisters. And brothers!" Adeline said, waving an open palm over a clutch of men in the crowd who shifted, uneasy at the unwanted attention. "The lies of the Prince of Lies! The promise of Satan himself and all within this scabby tent where men become as beasts and women as whores!"

The sisters murmured amens. Among them was the girl who was, only a week or more before, dancing naked on the bar of this very establishment. Now she wore the same modest white dress as the other sisters. Her hair combed and face scrubbed clean, she looked like a child. Her eyes were alight with the flame lit by Adeline's words.

"This place of sin, this *paradise*," Adeline said with the deepest scorn and derision, "is built upon the lowest floor of Hell. Its foundations rest on the suffering flesh of the damned who have heeded the promises and lies of the devil. But this house will not stand! This acre of Hell will be redeemed!"

Adeline ended her sermon by breaking into song, her voice sweet and clear in the early morning air.

When the last goodbye is spoken
And the tear stains wiped away…

She turned and entered the Paradise, parting a tent flap with her axe handle. The other sisters filed in behind, falling into "New Jerusalem" with her. The tent rang with their voices.

T.J. Bratt was not amused. Not at being awakened so early after going to bed. Not at his head still swollen with drink from the evening before. Not with discovering the dog-faced whore he'd chosen to lie with still in his bunk. And certainly not with his establishment infested with an army of pious bitches who showed no intention of departing.

He stormed out of his combination office/boudoir, taking only time to slip boots over bare feet, his further nakedness covered only by stained long johns.

"Stop that caterwauling! Stop it at once and get your fannies out of my saloon!" he pronounced in a voice that sounded to him like it was coming from the bottom of a well. The perils of cutting raisin jack with laudanum.

The women kept singing, lifting their voices higher to drown out the words of the vile man facing them.

"You are trespassers, and you will leave now!" he seethed between clenched teeth.

"We will do no such thing, Mr. Bratt!" Adeline proclaimed. "The Lord is not a trespasser. All is His kingdom, and we are free to spread his word within!"

"And thieves," Bratt shouted and rushed into the clutch of sisters to grab the wrist of the terrified girl who once whored in the Paradise. He yanked her free of the women. The girl's eyes grew wide in terror.

"You don't own her," Adeline proclaimed and brought down her axe handle onto Bratt's wrist with an audible crack. He released the girl's arm with a gargled cry.

"Damned I don't! I paid fifty dollars for her in Waco. Paid to bring her here on the train," Bratt said through twisted lips. He gripped his arm and winced, the flesh crimson and swelling. "She ain't near worked that off. Her cunny's as much mine as every bottle and jug in this place."

"You will have her over my dead body," Adeline said, and swatted at Bratt again. He stumbled back; eyes dark with fury.

"Bear!" he bawled. "Get your ragged ass on out here, Bear!"

The big man with the scarred face and mangled ears seemed to materialize from behind the roulette wheel. He stepped around the table; the stubby shotgun held easy in his fists.

"Now, unless you ladies want to meet Jesus this very morning then I suggest you hand back what's mine and move along out of here," Bratt said, his mouth curling up in a sneer.

"There's every chance you'll be seeing Jesus before the sisters," Joe Wiley said, stepping in from the sunlight, his .44 raised at T.J. Bratt's head.

"You can settle this, marshal. These women aren't paying customers," Bratt said, eyes locked on the deadly black eye of the revolver held steady at his nose.

"Of course," Joe said, ignoring Bratt's demands, "there's long odds on it being Jesus you'll see first. Unless He cares to come by and see you laying on the coals with the devil's pitchfork up your ass."

Some of the sisters gasped at Joe's words. A couple of them tittered at the image he conjured. Adeline met his gaze, her lips set together but eyes alive with amusement.

"This ain't fair, marshal. You know this ain't fair," Bratt said.

"Maybe it's not fair. But as far as this girl is concerned you no longer have claim," Joe said and cocked the hammer back on his pistol as he edged around to put T.J. between him and Bear. The owner of the Paradise was square in the middle of the firing line. His eyes swam back and forth, assessing his precarious situation.

"May I adjourn this meeting with your permission, Miss Adeline?" Joe said, eyes on the unmoving front blade of his .44, the barrel locked on Bratt's sweating face.

"You may, marshal," she said, her arms enfolding the terrified girl in a protective embrace.

"Go in peace, sisters," Joe said and backed toward the tent opening behind the gaggle of departing women, his pistol held out at the proprietor until all were clear and back on the street.

When they were in the sunlight once more Adeline Tibbets said, "You are the answer to a prayer, marshal."

"And you are a pain in my ass, ma'am," he said with a crooked smile as he offered her his arm. Together they followed after the procession of sisters marching back toward their revival tent singing "Are You Washed in the Blood?"

"Is there a way I can salve the wounds I have caused?" she said with the innocence of a lamb.

"I think you know the balm I prefer," he answered, eyes ahead, feeling her grip on his arm tighten.

"You're bone tired, son," Ben Temple said and blew a stream of smoke from his cigarillo. The creamy haze struck the board on the table between them making it appear as though the chess pieces were set in a swirling fog.

"And how's a blind man deduce that?" Joe said, his fingers hovering over the knob atop a pawn blocking the path of his own bishop.

"You're playing like a drunk Comanche or a fool," Ben said with scorn. "I'd get a better game out of one of those soakheads you have locked up over there."

Coolie Taylor slept on a bench before the locked cells. His snores competed with the racket from two cowboys sleeping it off in one cell and a travelling drummer they caught selling wood alcohol in the other.

"Well, I confess that my mind is on more pressing matters than rooks and queens," Joe said, feeling the past week of catnaps and hurried meals catching up with him.

"If it ain't sinners giving you hell it's the righteous offering you heaven."

"You heard about what happened down at the Paradise, huh?"

"Whole town's talking about it. And those that didn't see it themselves are getting an earful from those gabby sisters down at the temperance tent. But that's not what I was referring to, son."

"Then who's giving me all this heaven and hell you're on about?" Joe said, deciding to leave his pawn where it was and moving one of his knights from cover to threaten Ben's remaining rook.

"Those are thin walls over at the Grand Prairie," Ben said and swung a knight of his own out to take Joe's piece.

Joe's face reddened.

"You're in check, son," Ben said, his smile broadening.

"You win, old man," Joe said and tipped over his king. "I'm getting myself lunch and then sneaking a nap before the sun sets."

"Expecting more trouble tonight?" Ben said, drawing back the pieces to set up another game, white and black pieces in their place. Joe would never understand how a sightless man could manage that.

"Yeah," Joe said absently as he stood. "The Three Rivers is paying their hands today."

23

It was just as bad as Joe Wiley expected. In fact, it was worse.

He wasn't sure if it was because of a particularly good payoff for the cowboys or if they had been working too hard for too long. Or maybe they'd been owed back pay a while. Or perhaps it was something in the water.

Whatever the reason, Joe and his deputies were hard pressed to keep up with it all. The drovers off the Three Rivers poured into town and set to tearing it apart board and nail.

The Dugans, Coolie, and Joe rousted and ran in so many cowpokes that the jail was full to capacity. Joe had made a makeshift holding area in the livery stable. He had cowpokes in leg irons and chains secured to the roof beams. The blacksmith hammered rivets in place to secure the manacles to their ankles. Coolie held each man supported with one leg resting atop the anvil. Hungover and still half drunk, the drovers moaned with each strike of the hammer.

"This place stinks of horse shit!" a bedraggled cowpuncher moaned.

"It's gonna smell of *your* shit soon, buster. Ain't nobody running you to the privy," Coolie growled.

"What's stoppin' us from tearin' these chains loose?" another sorehead asked, giving his chain a tug.

"Be my guest. You're welcome to bring the whole damned roof down on the bunch of you," Joe said. "I suggest settling down and find a dry spot and sleep it off."

Joe turned to the livery caretaker. A cotton-haired older man named Pete, though due to his propensity to stutter was called Repeat. He was sitting on a comfy hay bale with an old Hawken Rifle across his lap. Repeat was rail thin but had outsized hands and wrists from years of swinging a hammer. The man looked like he'd been carved from a tree stump and left in the sun to dry. His eyes were hard and black under snow white brows.

"Repeat, if they so much as make a move to get out of that pen you put a hole through the first one," Joe said.

"Will do, mister marshal. Will do," Repeat repeated and spat a glob of tobacco juice onto the straw strewn floor. "It'd be my pleasure. My pleasure."

"I believe it will." Joe nodded with a hint of a smile.

All that evening and into the night found the lawmen dealing with one altercation or another. In the saloons, the streets, and once in a bath house when there was an argument over who was next to wash the filth of the trail off of themselves. Two other fights broke out over the pecking order at one of the whore tents.

"Goldamn!" Coolie Taylor said. "This is worse than fighting Yankees!"

"How you figure that?" Seth Dugan asked.

"At least the Yankees would just kill ya and get it over with or run away back to Philadelphia," Coolie explained. "This is like herding chickens or unruly brats. And it's thirsty work."

"I grant ya that," Seth agreed before laying out a cowboy with a bone shattering elbow.

Just when Joe thought they might have finally got the tiger by the tail he witnessed Adeline Tibbets and the sisters of the Holy Crusade Committee marching toward the Paradise once again armed with axe handles and torches. He'd seen them stern and angry before but there was something different in their stride, something purposeful and menacing. They weren't going to the Paradise to preach. This was a Jesus and the money changers moment. This was a retribution and a reckoning. He hurried to catch up to them with Coolie in tow. They came up alongside Adeline who was staring ahead, her face a mask of righteous fury.

"Where's the fire, Sister?" Joe asked hoping to quell her fervor.

"That man took her, marshal. That filthy pig of a man took Sister Hester back to his den of iniquity, his seraglio. We mean to take her back!" Adeline said.

"The little who—the little redhead? You sure she was took?" Joe asked. He also wondered what a seraglio was.

"I know how dubious you are of Sister Hester's redemption. But I assure you she was one of us. She heard The Word and The Truth and turned her back on sin. Then that animal came like a thief in the night for her," Adeline said. Her eyes bored holes through Joe. "His brute accosted her and took her back to Bratt to be used for his benefit. We will not allow that to happen, marshal."

"All due respect, ma'am," Coolie said, "but them axe handles ain't gonna help much against guns. I know this type of human trash from personal experience. They'd as soon shoot you as say hello if they think they can get away with it."

"And you being ladies won't slow Bratt's hand even a little. Let me handle it, Adeline," Joe said, hand on her shoulder. "It's my job. And I don't want you and the rest of the sisters getting hurt. I'll get her back for you."

Adeline regarded him, eyes searching his face. She sighed and nodded.

"Very well. But if you fail, we are resolved in this. Sister Hester is one of us and we are charged with her protection and well-being. We will do what we must to make certain of that," Adeline said.

Joe looked Adeline in the eyes. Conveying his feelings through his gaze and the soft pressure of his hand on the fabric covering her shoulder.

"That's fair enough. But I won't fail. I promise you that." Joe let his hand fall away from Adeline with reluctance and turned to Coolie. "Let's go."

Joe and Coolie closed ground towards the Paradise. Inside, the place was foggy with smoke and packed side to side with drovers, drummers and others who drifted into town to celebrate the end of the roundup. The marshal and deputy were greeted by T.J. Bratt standing behind the bar. The lumbering Bear beside him clutched the terrified Sister Hester with an iron grip on her slim wrist. Her eyes were glassy with drink. A half empty bottle rested on the bar before her. Her white dress was in tatters, a sleeve torn away and the front ripped down to reveal her breasts. A black weal was swelling under one eye.

Her reintroduction to her former life of sin was in progress.

"Welcome, marshal. We've been expecting you," Bratt said. A cocky sneer on his smug face.

"We?" Joe asked. Not liking the bravado Bratt was showing one tiny bit.

"We," Big Cal Randall said as he emerged from the crowd with a brace of men from the Twisted Tree ranch. "Good evening, marshal."

"Damned if it is," Coolie said.

It was an ambush. Joe cursed himself for a fool.

"We have some unfinished business, marshal," Big Cal said ominously.

24

There were no threats exchanged. No idle boasts of death-dealing skill. No insults. No promises of terrible violence to come. No one working up their nerve or getting their blood hot with words. There was none of that ginning up of courage that men intent on murder often engage in before the killing starts.

Joe cleared both holsters in the blink of an eye. His hands were empty and then they were full. And when they were full, they both spat fire. A man either side of Big Cal dropped to the floor. Cal threw himself back into the crowd of men, emptying his holsters as he fell.

Coolie turned his shotgun toward T.J. Bratt behind the bar. He bent to a crouch and let fly with both barrels. The double load took out one of the kegs holding the bar top up. It collapsed in a storm of wood shards and shattering glass. Bratt stumbled back into the racks of bottles, bringing up his own scatter gun.

Bear yanked the little redhead toward him by the wrist. Somehow, she broke free and tumbled to the floor.

Big Cal was rolling over the sand and sawdust seeking to hide under the roulette table. Joe followed him at a walk, blazing away with both pistols booming.

Bratt sent an answering charge of buckshot and tacks from this scattergun. Coolie leapt aside. A pair of drovers took the loads in the legs and fell screaming. Coolie rolled to his belly, revolver drawn and firing shots blind through the pall of white smoke and swirling sawdust.

Half the patrons of the Paradise fled through the tent flaps or crawled out under the canvas walls. The rest stayed either to see the rest of the show, too drunk to know better, or joined the fight on the side of their cowboy brothers. The air became alive with lead flying in every direction but mostly toward the pair of lawmen now separated by ten feet of open space.

Joe wheeled and gunned a man raising a rifle at Coolie's back. He struck the man in the back of the head. The drover fell flopping, a new mouth open where his nose used to be. Coolie was up on his feet firing into the clouds of smoke toward the bar until his Remington went dry. A pair of drovers lay dead at his feet. Joe was at his side, tossing off his .32 into Coolie's empty left hand. They were back-to-back now with the cowboys closing in a half ring about them. The shots were dying away now, the last going through the canvas above, fired without aim or caution by men too scared or too drunk to be any real good in a fight.

Spinning his Colt in his hand, Joe held the weapon by the barrel. The searing heat came through his leather glove. He laid about the heads of the encircling pack. They dropped as if poleaxed with each swing of his arm. He thought of Samson cracking Philistine skulls with the jawbone of an ass. Not much had changed since the days of the prophets. The men melted before him as they saw their brothers spilling to the floor with smashed noses and ruined mouths. Coolie moved with him, reloading his pistol and glaring into the smoky gloom.

"Joe, the girl," Coolie said behind him.

Joe spared a glance to the floor before the bar. A tiny shape lay still there. A dark crimson stain spread across her once-fine embroidered dress of virginal white. He plied the butt of his Colt against the temple of a sneering drover with added fury and smiled as he felt the wet crunch of collapsing bone through the blue steel of the barrel in his fist.

A gasp and high squeal of feminine voices made Joe turn from his work. Adeline stood aghast before a phalanx of her sisters now crowded in the tent opening. Their eyes were locked on the fallen angel lying dead on the filthy barroom floor, never to sin again. Some of them wailed in terror. Others turned their heads away. Only Adeline remained cold-eyed and calm, the kind of calm Joe knew could turn to a sudden storm.

"Cover my back!" Joe called and crossed the Paradise in three strides to lay hands on Adeline and push her and her sisters back out onto the street. Coolie backed up toward the exit, his Remington turning back and forth to cover the remaining cowboys moving to follow.

He didn't see Big Cal snake-crawl, unharmed, from under the roulette table with its heavy marble top fractured from .44 slugs.

Cal fired from a prone position lying on his belly, pistol trained on Coolie stepping backward through the flap. A slug took Coolie low in the gut, folding him over. A second punched through a thigh and the deputy buckled in the heap. A third, fired by Big Cal up on one knee now, split Coolie's skull like a melon. The man dropped to the floor, lifeless but for one twitching boot gouging at the sand with its heel.

The cowboy stepped over the deputy's body to make his way through the flap into the cool night of the street. Those that could still stand and still walk, followed behind to see how all this was going to play out.

Cal caught up with the marshal in the center of the street. Joe Wiley turned at the gunshots from within the Paradise in time to see Cal stepping toward him, grinning, the big revolver wavering in his direction.

"I had your deputy and now I'm gonna have you, lawman," Cal said, childish mirth in his voice. "Then I'm gonna have that pretty bitch behind you. Gonna ride her over a barrel till the sun rises."

Joe felt Adeline stiffen with a hiss behind him. He reached a hand back to hold her in place.

"You got me flat, Cal," Joe said and relaxed his hand to drop the empty Colt to the dirt. The butt was matted with the hair and blood of the men he'd buffaloed.

"I do indeed," Cal said and worked the hammer back, barrel trained on the badge on Joe's vest.

"Do me one favor and let the ladies step clear. You have a story to tell your grandchildren. Don't spoil it by killing any innocent women," Joe said, low and smooth. He was gratified to feel Adeline step away from the touch of his fingers, retreating with the other sisters.

"Fair enough," Cal said. The pistol wavered as he waited until the street behind the marshal was clear.

"Mind if I say a prayer, cowboy?" Joe said, fingers touching the silver crucifix dangling from the loop of chain at his waist.

"If you think it would help," Cal said, eyes crinkling in amusement.

"Oh, I do." Joe yanked the chain and a small derringer at the end popped from the watch pocket on this vest. It was in his hand with blinding speed and held straight armed at Big Cal's face. The derringer exploded with a boom surprising for the size of the tiny pistol. Joe's arm flew upwards with the wicked kick of the stubby piece.

The single .30 carbine slug drove through Cal's right eye to explode out of the back of his skull in a shower of blood, bone and greasy brain stuff. The little cowboy stumbled back a pace on his heels. His revolver swung loose at the end of his arm and discharged into the dirt just before he crashed like a pine plank to the street.

"Anyone else?" Joe said through clamped teeth and spun the smoking midget gun at the withdrawing crowd of drovers. The derringer was empty—only they didn't know that for certain.

He looked past the dispersing pack of cowboys to see T.J. Bratt standing spread-legged on the boardwalk of the Paradise, his coach gun cradled in one arm and Bear looming behind him. The ends of

Bratt's mustache danced as the grin on his face broke open to show yellowed teeth.

"See what you wrought, marshal? You brung all this down on your own head. No one to blame but yourself."

Joe stooped to retrieve his Colt and recalled that his .32 still lay in Coolie's hand inside the Paradise.

He promised himself he'd be back to retrieve it once he saw Adeline and the sisters back safe to their revival tent.

25

"I liked Coolie. He made me laugh," Seth Dugan said. He broke open a box of ten-gauge cartridges on the desk top.

"I known you all my life, brother. Never seen you laugh once," Len said as he scooped up stubby shells and stuffed them in his pockets.

"Made me smile then," Seth said, glowering.

Len shrugged and let the matter go.

Joe Wiley stood in the open doorway of the jail house and watched the pair check the loads on their shotguns.

"You boys know what we're about to do," he said.

"We're putting down some mad dogs, is all," Len said. The brothers joined him out on the boardwalk.

"Me and anyone else wearing a badge is going to become plain unpopular in Mercury Wells after tonight," Joe said.

"I got all the friends I need," Seth said. He set out down the street toward the Paradise. The other two followed, taking long strides to keep up.

The brothers entered the tent behind a fiery storm of double-ought. Len let both barrels fly toward the bar. One of the keeps was on hands and knees mopping up blood. He was chopped down in a blizzard of shot and flying splinters. Wild shot crashing from the smooth bore barrels turned bottles above the bar into a lethal sleet of glass.

Seth followed behind; his own scattergun raised while his brother crouched to reload. Bear emerged from the gloom, an ax handle held back for a swing. A charge of buck removed his head at the neck in an explosion of flesh and bone. The big bruin of a man flopped to the floor, legs dancing. Seth swung the shotgun across the room. Cowboys, startled to sudden sobriety, rolled and tumbled to cover in all directions. Seth discharged his remaining barrel from the hip to keep them on the prod. Cowboys belly-crawled under the walls of the tent to escape the carnage. The canvas flapped like a ship's sail in a stiff blow with the force of their hasty exit.

The Dugans stood in the gun smoke stink with shotguns covering all the remaining company. Two surviving bartenders stood with shaking hands open before them. T.J. Bratt came around from the back of his gaming table with hands before him and fingers spread. He glanced down at the headless heap of his loyal bodyguard. A shadow of regret moved across his face. He came to a stop by the body of Coolie Taylor still lying dead where he fell in the filthy sawdust.

"Am I to suppose that I am under arrest?" Bratt said with a trace of a smile curling his lip.

Marshal Joe Wiley came through the tent flies, Colt drawn. He parted the Dugan brothers to level the big revolver inches from Bratt's nose.

"That my weapon?" Joe said, eyes cutting to Bratt's vest front. His .32 was tucked in the man's waistband.

Bratt nodded, gaze lowered. "You're free to retrieve it, marshal."

"I'd prefer you hand it to me."

Bratt's eyes leapt up to regard Joe Wiley's level stare. His mouth fell slack. A fresh film of sweat sprang to Bratt's face.

"That's not to my liking. I am surrendering myself to your custody, marshal. Let the wheels of justice grind fine and slow." His grin returned; his eyes narrowed.

"Not for you," Joe said. The big Colt barked. A fat slug cleaved T.J. Bratt's skull in two. A spray of bone and brain showered behind the man. He stumbled back one step, then two, before folding to the floor in a lifeless sprawl.

"Out," Joe growled to the surviving bartenders. They scrambled through the tent opening, skirting the Dugans on their way to the street. He stooped to yank his .32 from Bratt's belt.

"Let's get our friend out of this shithole," Joe said. Seth handed his shotgun off to his brother and crouched to take the body of their friend under the arms. He rose with Coolie slung over his shoulder.

Behind the bar Joe found a can of lamp oil. He poured it over the floor, splashing it into the spreading pool of liquor from bottles shattered by the Dugans' opening salvos.

"Better step outside, boys," Joe said, taking a glass lamp down from a hook.

Out on the street a new crowd was gathering. They watched Seth Dugan emerge carrying the still form of Coolie Taylor. Len Dugan stepped from the walk with a shotgun in each fist. Marshal Wiley was the last out. He tossed the lit glass lamp back into the tent. A ball of orange flame tinged in black rushed from within. Inside of seconds the sprawling tent was consumed, canvas flapping to send sparks flying. The crowd receded from a sudden wall of furnace heat. A tower of black smoke rose to smear the stars away.

Joe stepped between the Dugans, a Colt to each hand.

"This was a reckoning! A reckoning!" He spoke loud to be heard over the whoosh and gutter of the inferno behind him. The crowd shifted as more joined the throng, coming from the tents and saloons.

The mayor came through the mob followed by some of the other town founders. His honor wore no collar, and his vest was unbuttoned. Such was his hurry to reach the conflagration. His face was red with fury even in the crimson light of the burning Paradise.

"Mister Wiley!" he thundered. Joe noted that the mayor did not refer to him by his title.

"Not tonight, mayor! I won't hear from you tonight! This ain't politics. This is between my men and anyone who would break the law."

The mayor stepped back, swallowing hard, his own rage forgotten in the face of the marshal's wrath.

"Anyone else who breaks the law in Mercury Wells can expect the same from me and my deputies!" Joe went on, his voice a guttural roar. "I will not tolerate a town where a lawman's life is considered forfeit. Force will be met with force. That's my word. That's my law."

He turned his back on the faces gleaming in the glow of the rising flames. A figure in white stood apart from the others. Adeline's eyes gleamed wet with tears. He took a step toward her but she turned to shimmer away into a pall of smoke swirling over the street.

26

The grass shone with the crystalline glimmer of dew still clinging to stalks yet untouched by the rays of the rising sun. Where the sunlight spread its reach, a fine mist drifted and eddied above the tips of the carefully manicured lawn that stretched all about the mansion seated above the banks of Lake Michigan.

The limping man made his way to a patch of level lawn and stooped to set a round white ball atop a small pile of sand. He steadied himself to reach out a gloved hand. An extraordinarily tall man, a Sikh, stepped forward to hold out a wooden club selected from a selection in a bag slung from a broad shoulder. The limping man examined the wooden shaft that ended in a carved club with one side planed at a flat angle. He nodded in approval without a glance back at the Sikh.

Despite his infirmity, one leg shorter than the other and unsatisfactorily compensated for with a custom-built shoe with a raised sole and heel, the limping man swung the club with practiced skill. The club struck the ball square and sent the ivory-colored orb on a long arc to rest out of sight over a grassy hummock.

On his way to the final destination of the ball he'd launched, the limping man was greeted by men hailing him as they trotted across the lawn on a path of interception.

"What nonsense is this?" the limping man said to himself. The Sikh stood awaiting further instruction. Resting in the leather golf bag was a Nitro Express gaming gun charged with rounds the size of bananas. Should the master desire his round not be interrupted, the Sikh was ready, at a nod, to deploy both lethal barrels in the direction of the trespassers.

The limping man stood leaning on his club to await the new arrivals' approach. Four men huffed and puffed over the grass, fine shoes slick with morning damp.

"John Delano has been forced to resign," said the man in the lead while the others recovered their breath.

"The President's brother as well!" another managed to gasp out.

"And what would cause the Interior Secretary to do such a thing?" the limping man said.

"The land grants. Surely, it's the land grants. If he's quit, they must have discovered the bogus nature of the land grants we purchased through your syndicate," a third man said, the rasp in his voice ill concealing the quaver of terror there.

"And Orvil Grant as well. It has to be his efforts for us in Indian Affairs. All our work through the Indian attorneys to secure the parcels required for our expansion scheme," the fourth man said, either calm or resigned.

"You have arrived at a crucial point in time, gentlemen," the limping man said in a grave voice.

The others leaned forward as one to learn the full import of this moment.

"I am two down on my usual score with two holes remaining," the limping man said.

The others looked to one another, perplexed.

"So, if you will continue your sad tale as we walk to my man there," the limping man said, setting off up the gentle slope of the hillock towards where the Sikh stood solid as a sentry over the place where the ball had fallen.

The quartet followed and explained in full the news from the capitol, their narrative broken only by silent interludes while the limping man took his shots, long strokes and putts, to close out the last two holes. These men were, in no certain order of importance, a United

States senator, the governor of Illinois, the owner of a consortium of railroad lines, and the president of a bank with branches in New York, Chicago, St. Louis and New Orleans. And yet, these men, who could move millions of dollars and thousands of citizens with a snap of their fingers, chased the limping man over his lawn while he chased a little white pill across the grass.

They explained to the limping man that the land grants they finagled through payments to the Interior Secretary had been revealed as phony. None had gone through the usual lanes of bureaucracy or been approved through proper channels. The transactions had been facilitated by so-called Indian attorneys who, as it was now known to the public, were charlatans and shills paid eight dollars a day in taxpayer money to represent the various native tribes in legal purchases of tribal land. In truth these "attorneys" had no more contact with any Indians than the Queen of the Netherlands. They were simply hacks hired to rubber stamp land grants of dubious provenance. These "attorneys" were overseen by Orvil Grant, brother to the President of the United States.

The grants had been engineered by the men currently in pursuit of the limping man through a syndicate formed by the limping man. They included millions of acres of land rich in mineral deposits as well as the rights of way for rail tracks needed to deliver those goods from the wastelands of the west to the markets of the east and beyond.

At the conclusion of their story and his game, the limping man stood at the final hole and marked down figures in a leather-clad notebook. He closed the book with a wintery smile and replaced it in the pocket of his vest.

The senator made to speak but the limping man held up a hand to shush him. A servant, a balding man in black livery and tie, was crossing the lawn in their direction. He bore a silver tray. Upon the tray, perfectly balanced, was a tall tumbler of iced water with one half of a fresh lemon squeezed in it. By the sweating glass was a telegram folded in two.

The limping man took the cold glass with chilly gratitude and the telegram with marked disdain.

The telegram informed him of mounting concerns over the behavior of law enforcement agents in a place called Mercury Wells.

The limping man frowned deeply, folded the telegram in four and stuffed it in his pocket by his scorebook. He dashed the lemon water to the lawn and stomped on the glass with his raised shoe. It was crushed underfoot with a sound like a pistol shot. He turned without a word to walk to the palatial house along the lake. The liveried servant and the giant Sikh followed.

The four men stood on the wet lawn and looked to one another, left to wonder what could draw a man's attention away from his part in the biggest scandal in decades.

27

Joe Wiley, Ben Temple, and Len and Seth Dugan sat around the small jailhouse in the shuddering light of an oil lamp. They were sharing the last pot of coffee Coolie Taylor made in his lifetime. The contemplative silence was finally broken by Ben Temple who swallowed down another mouthful and winced.

"He made a lousy pot of coffee, but I wish he were around to make more of it."

Joe nodded and moved to the jailhouse window. He looked out on the dark town illuminated by a smattering of oil lamps strung up along the street. A fog hung over the street from the smoldering remains of the Paradise.

"We'll have to find someone to take his place. More than one maybe. Three or four. We're going to have a lot of men moving against us," Joe said.

"How about 'Pepper Belly' Santos? He's a pain in the ass Mex but he's a wildcat in a fight," offered Seth.

"That Englishman Reginald Wells-Upson is in Abilene. He's a crack shot when he's not drinking," Len suggested.

"How about we get out before you make any more new enemies?" Ben reasoned. Hoping against hope that Joe would heed his suggestion.

"You know I can't do that, Ben." Joe shook his head and moved to his desk where Ben was seated.

"And why the hell not?" Ben asked staring into nothingness.

Joe sat on the edge of the desk, contemplating his cup and the black sludge inside it.

"I don't leave a job unfinished. I don't run from a fight. I don't take the law lightly. Nor my word once given. And I mean to not have Coolie Taylor to have died for nothing," Joe said, voice low almost as if in prayer.

"Well, you're a fool. Always have been," Ben said.

Joe straightened. He dashed the contents of his cup to the floor and strode over the board to stand before Ben Temple.

"You're free to leave any time, old man. You say the word and I'll get the Texas and New Orleans boy to take your arm and lead you to the station," he said.

"You know I won't. You count on that, *lean* on that. Only I'm telling you that you're leading us all down the path to Perdition," Ben said. His unseeing eyes locked on where he believed Joe's face to be.

"You'd know a thing or two about that," Joe said, the edge coming off his voice.

The blind man made no reply to that. But Ben Temple knew, as he figured the Dugans did as well, that Joe Wiley's main reason for staying in Mercury Wells was Sister Adeline Tibbets—despite what he said. But that entered personal territory that one man doesn't enter into with another man, even one that's been like a son to you.

Len Dugan moved to take his turn to look out the window and witnessed Mayor Geoffrey Tuchman and Bob Miller approaching the jailhouse. They were in the lead of a phalanx of townsmen.

"Heads up. The mayor and that milksop constable is headed this way with some sore headed citizens," Len warned.

"Let 'em come," Joe said.

The mayor arrived at the jailhouse door and reached out to bang on it angrily. He was robbed of that satisfaction by Len Dugan opening it even as the mayor's fist fell on open air.

"Evening, Your Honor." Len insincerely doffed his bowler.

The mayor glared at Len and then Seth and then walked past them to Joe Wiley with Miller on his heels. The remaining men waited on the boardwalk or scattered in the street.

"Do your duty, Constable," the mayor said hotly. He stabbed at Joe Wiley with a trembling finger. Rage maybe. Or fear. Or both.

Bob Miller strode up to Joe Wiley like a peacock ready to spread his feathers.

"I am charging your two goons for murder and I am riding to the county seat to bring back constables to see that they answer to those charges," Miller threatened.

"I reckon you can't do that six feet under the ground," Seth said as he moved toward Miller.

"Seth! Don't you do it!" Joe ordered.

Seth considered it for a moment and then receded but looked Bob Miller in the eyes. It was the look a predator has when gazing on his next meal.

"I want you to know, Bob Miller, that Joe Wiley just saved your life. For now," Seth Dugan said, voice level and cold.

"This is precisely the problem. You are making a shambles of my town and a mockery of the law. This is not what I hired you to do. This will not stand. You haven't an idea of what sort of trouble you have brought yourself, Mr. Wiley. But it will not end well for you," Mayor Tuchman said with fury. His large frame shook.

Joe stood up to face Bob Miller and the mayor.

"I think the both of you had better leave. Do what you think you have to do. But get out of our sight," Joe warned.

"Heed my words well," the mayor added and turned on his heels and left the building with Bob following but turning so as not to put his back to Seth Dugan. The corner of Seth's mouth showed teeth.

"I wonder what he meant by all that?" Len asked.

"He sure was riled," Seth said.

"Maybe he intends to message Austin to send in the Rangers. You put a thought to that?" Ben said.

Joe shook his head.

"No Rangers. But surely something else. And not just angry, Seth. Scared. He's also scared. Hard to tell what a frightened man might do."

"And what the hell's all this mystery about us not having any idea what brand of trouble we're in?" Len said.

"Just hot air," Joe said.

"You're wrong, Joe," Ben said, placing a hand on the chair back to rise. "I heard it in his voice. He was yellow-shit scared talking to you like that. But the one time he talked like he was on solid ground was that threat. 'You haven't an idea of what sort of trouble you have brought yourself, Mr. Wiley.' Those words meant something."

Joe walked over to look out the barred window of the small jail again. His mind worked at what he had gotten himself into. And he knew that if he were a smart man, he'd heed Ben's words and clear out of this place. But he knew deep down he couldn't do that. Wouldn't do that. So, what would be, would be. Whatever the days that were to come brought him, he was going to go down fighting.

A lowing sound, growing louder, caused him to look toward the train station. Something moved there in the early morning gloom. A large shape, dark against the dawn shadows and growing to fill the street from side to side. Beneath his booted feet a tremble reached him through the floorboards.

It was cattle, a few thousand head, stampeding out of the stock-yard.

28

Furious over the Paradise incident and the death of Big Cal, riders from the Twisted Tree ranch pulled a long length of fence from the pens. Using rope flails and shots from their rifles, they encouraged a panic that sent a rush of cattle up the center of Mercury Wells. Two thousand head or more in a blind rush.

The animals, mad with fear, funneled into the main street. Thousands of tons of live, enraged, terrified Texas steers drove straight into the heart of the town. They crowded flank to flank, fighting to find open sky beyond the enclosure of the buildings and tents hemming them in either side. The beeves climbed boardwalks, their weight bringing down uprights. The front façade of the Dollar Store was sent crashing into the street, crushing the bones of two steers and driving the rest to a higher frenzy.

With a shower of shattered glass, the front windows of a sutler's store imploded. Steers were crowded onto the boardwalk, goring one another to fight their way clear. A half dozen sought the interior of the store as refuge. They trod barrels and shelves to splinters. The wooden staircase to the second floor buckled and fell under their assault. The sutler's family stood horror-struck at the top of the stairs, clutching one another in fright, to witness their once going enterprise turned to worthless debris.

A thunderous cacophony of beating hooves and cracking timber filled the air as tent after tent and shack after shack were torn down under the surge of senseless beasts. Screams arose above the rumble of their passage. A steer, its horns snagged in a tent line, ran about in ever decreasing circles with a bloodied nightgown tangled under one hoof. Somewhere in the collection of tents, a swatch of canvas was splashed with the oil from a smashed lamp. A blaze rose and swiftly spread, the flames stirring up the fear in the cattle to new heights. The beeves were shrieking now, mad with terror.

They swept down the street for open country where they spread out in all directions as though to race their own shadows to the mountains just turning gold under the rays of the rising sun.

When the bovine tide finally passed the ruin was terrible. A wide swath of Mercury Wells was destroyed, either trampled to wreckage or burning. Bodies, barely recognizable as human lay crushed into the dust of the street. A few wounded beeves thrashed out the last of their lives until put down by men with guns. Wails of despair and cries of anguish echoed off the fronts of the buildings that remained.

And at far edge of town lay the sad remains of the Holy Crusade Committee tent. A few poles still stood, shreds of canvas hanging to flap in the breeze. The rest of the tent, and its contents, had been stamped to rubbish under thousands of hooves.

At the center of the destruction, Adeline Tibbets was on her knees weeping over the trampled bodies of two of her sisters. She was surrounded by a ring of her followers holding hands with heads lowered.

29

As the townspeople, awakened by the havoc of the stampede, began to pick up the pieces and the bodies left in the wake of the catastrophe, Joe Wiley gathered his deputies together. Ben Temple stood with them.

Joe Wiley surveyed the damage and carnage. He ground his teeth. He spied one cow that ended up trampled by its fellow cattle and walked over to it. He hunched down and took a close look at its brand. He stood and walked back to his deputies and mentor with eyes cold as the grave.

"This was no accident. That steer is from Twisted Tree. My wager is that all of them are."

"Holy hell," Len Dugan said, and his brother Seth whistled low in response.

"I don't suppose I'll waste my breath again and suggest that we leave now," Ben Temple said as much to himself as to Joe Wiley. It was just as well since Joe ignored him.

"They'll likely still be at the stockyards. You two swing around the other side of the station house and meet me there," Joe ordered.

Joe walked on a direct course to the stockyards, across the tracks to the stock pens. Cowboys lounged about leaning on posts and roosting on rails. There were six drovers from the Twisted Tree, but they weren't alone. A group of cowpokes from the Three Rivers was there as well. Hector Nostrand was in company with them. The boss man was wearing a tailored suit of fawn colored whipcord under his broad-brimmed Stetson. He looked like a picture postcard character.

"I mean to take these men to jail, and I won't brook any interference," Joe announced.

"And you are taking them to jail for what cause, marshal?" Nostrand asked. He stepped before the gang of drovers.

"Yeah. We ain't done shit," said one of the accused. A man called Billy Caruthers. His fellows chimed in with their own protestations.

Joe bristled at their brass. They thought they had numbers on him. It gave them courage a mile wide and an inch deep.

"That stampede was no accident. It was deliberate and I believe these six men set it in motion." His gesture took in Caruthers and the other Twisted Tree men.

"Myself and my men can assure you that it was a terrible accident. And I will do my part to aid the community of Mercury Wells to deal with this unforeseen tragedy," Nostrand said. His manner was imperious. He fully expected Joe to back down.

Joe shook his head.

"This has gone beyond you and your fat wallet, mister. If what you say is true, then it will come out in the trial. But I know what's true and I mean to see these men hang for the murder of those sisters and other poor souls in town."

"You have no proof," Nostrand said, taking another step to place himself square between Joe and the Twisted Tree crew. Homer Gibbs stepped away from the fence to back his boss's play.

"I have a damn sight enough proof to make an arrest. I have the brands on the cattle. And I'm betting I'll find rails down on the pens with nary a hoof mark on them. You'd best step clear or I'll run you in too," Joe said. His left hand rested easy at his side, fingers relaxed just below his holstered Colt.

"You can try, marshal," Nostrand said. He broke into an open smile at the sound of spurs and creak of leather telling him he had an armed company behind him to give his words menace.

"Seth. Len. Move 'em along," Joe said, eyes outside the half circle of armed men.

The Dugans came along the tracks, shotguns directed at the clutch of drovers turning to regard them.

"You heard the man," Seth said, standing firm, the double barrels unwavering at his hip.

"No sudden moves," Len said.

"You are making a very serious mistake, Wiley. If I am against you, the Three Rivers is against you. That means the town is against you. Railroad too," Nostrand said, face reddening.

"The law and God, Nostrand. It's all I've ever really had at my back," Joe said as he backed up, hands easy at his sides.

The six Twisted Tree hands were cut from the group. The surrendered their weapons to Joe under the vigilant eye of the Dugans. They marched to the jailhouse in a procession watched by half the population. Joe led the way, his back to the men and arms loaded with their gun belts. The Dugans brought up the rear, scatter guns leveled at the six prisoners.

When they reached the jail house, they saw that the front had been written on with whitewash paint. Emblazoned across the front was the simple epitaph: KILLERS

"Well look at that," Billy Caruthers said with a chuckle. "Seems like there is some disagreement as to who are the killers and who ain't."

"Shut up." Seth drove the butt of his shotgun into the man's side. Carruthers dropped, sucking air.

Joe stepped onto the boardwalk before the jailhouse. The severed head of a steer lay propped against the door. Silver-backed flies swarmed over the hide and gathered in the corners of its dead eyes.

He then noticed several townsfolk standing around watching silently. Knowing they must have seen who performed the vandalism, he spoke up.

"Anyone see who done this?" he asked. The silence remained.

"I didn't think so," he said with disdain and kicked the head into the street before leading his prisoners inside.

30

Once the six out of the Twisted Tree were locked up, three to a cell, Joe Wiley turned to the Dugans.

"This thing is getting hairy. I can't expect the two of you to see this through at this point. You're free to cut out."

"The Dugan brothers don't cut out on a fight. We told you that. You bring it up one more time I'll set you on your ass so's you remember it," Len Dugan said. Shaking his head with a sour look.

"You know better than that, Joe," Seth Dugan added.

Joe stepped to them, face grim.

"You see what's going on out there? These damned cowboys just about stampeded this town flat, but the good citizens still hate us more. And what was our crime? Trying to bring some order to this shithole town of theirs?"

"You looking for a gold medal and town picnic in our honor?" Seth said and made a face as near to a smile as anyone would ever see on his face.

Seated behind the desk Ben Temple spoke up.

"And don't bother asking me to leave. Even though I think you're a damned fool I ain't going anywhere. I heard that commotion outside. But I didn't see a thing with these damned eyes. I did get a whiff of a tobacco. Rare stuff. I've only smelled it once before but it's unmistakable. Damned if I can recall where I smelt it first though."

"Never mind. You three stay here. I'm going to have a look around," Joe said and left the jail.

After the door slammed shut Ben grunted, "He means check on that Sister Adeline."

Joe walked down the main street looking from side to side to survey the damage. He kept an eye out for anyone from either of the big ranches. He stopped where the Holy Crusade tent had been only to find Sister Adeline Tibbets and her followers packing their wagons to depart.

"Where are you going?" Joe asked.

"Far away from here, marshal. Far, far away," Adeline answered. Her eyes were red. Her pretty face was drawn and pale under a powder of fine ash.

"Giving up?" he asked her, his heart in his throat.

"I have lost three of my sisters. You lost your friend. And those aren't all that have paid the price for this madness. This place is beyond redemption. It has descended into the pit and you, you, marshal, are a part of it. You think you are standing against hell fire but all you are doing is stoking the coals. So, yes, I am giving up. I know you won't. And even more than watching this town destroy itself, I do not want to watch you destroy yourself. Goodbye, Joseph." Adeline touched his cheek with her fingers.

He gripped her wrist, holding it there.

"I don't want you to go," he said.

"I'm tired, Joe. Tired to my soul. This town has cost me too much and I'm leaving," she said. Her eyes pleaded with him.

His grip tightened.

"Come with me," she whispered, lips barely parted.

He released her then.

Her eyes darkened. The tightness around them went slack. She dropped her hand from his face and turned to the wagons. With the help of the sisters, she climbed onto the driver's bench of the front wagon.

She gave him one last mournful gaze and then hit the reins. The leather straps slapped the backs of the mules in their traces.

"Get 'em up."

The mules lunged; the wagon's wheels broke into a roll. The Holy Crusade rode north out of Mercury Wells.

Joe held his silence. He watched bitterly as they, as *she*, left. The yellow dust rose behind the wagons. When it had blown clear the wagons were gone, invisible over the horizon, gone deep into the grazing lands. His resolve was now forged in steel. No one was going to take this town away from him—even if he had to level it to the ground.

"Just as well," he muttered.

Joe's dark reflections were blasted away by the report of gunfire back from the center of town. He headed at a run toward the jailhouse.

31

A man lay breathing his last in the street. A reedy little man Joe knew to be a pimp named Ollie Nielson.

Blood pooled below him from two fresh holes in his chest. A Remington revolver lay by his quavering hand. Further along a cowboy leaned on a hitch rail for support, a crimson stain running down one leg of his chaps from a ragged hole punched in the leather. A pal stood by him offering words of comfort and sips from a bottle. A third drover stepped to the downed pimp, rifle in hand. He walked with a purpose, working the lever to jack a new round into the rifle's chamber.

"He's done. Leave him be," Joe said, walking with right hand raised toward the angry drover.

"Just proddin' him along," the approaching man growled.

The drover raised his Winchester but not before Joe had cleared leather. The rifleman was staring into the steady gaze of the marshal over the barrel of the raised Colt. He let the rifle drop to his side, hand back on the neck of the buttstock away from the trigger. "He had no cause, marshal," the drover said, voice husky with rage.

"No cause?" Joe scoffed. "You run a herd through town and trampled a bunch of his whores to raspberry jam. Man had a right to his redemption."

"That was Twisted Tree beef. We're Three Rivers."

"I guess Nielson wasn't feeling particular this morning."

"You holding us, marshal?"

Joe looked about him to see folks stopped in the work of clearing away the wreckage of the morning. They stood watching the tableau before them. One man dead or nearly so. Another holed through the leg. The marshal, alone on the street, standing in judgement. Joe Wiley sighed and dropped his Colt back in place on his hip.

"Looks like self-defense to me. Get your friend to a surgeon," he said. He continued to the jailhouse where the Dugans stood waiting on the front walk.

"Get the hell off the street," he growled. The brothers stepped back into the jailhouse. Joe joined them.

"We heard shooting," Les said.

"And both of you went to look making both of you targets," Joe said. "From now on there's two men watching the cells all the time. Come nights we all fort up in here."

"Well, I'll be goddamned if I'm going to sit in here 'round the clock smelling your farts," Ben Temple said, rising from his chair.

"Nobody deputized you, Ben," Joe said.

Ben stopped before Joe, placing a hand on the marshal's arm.

"Even a blind man can see you're in over your head here, son. Maybe a blind man sees it better than most." Ben didn't wait for a reply but turned and made it through the door unaided into the sun blasted street.

Joe stood in the bar of light cast on the floor and watched the old man make his way across the street toward the Majestic.

"I'm going to the telegraph office to send out some invites," Joe said.

"You so sure we're still on the town payroll?" Les said.

"I have a contract. Iron bound," Joe said, turning to the brothers once he saw Ben had made it safe to the opposite boardwalk.

"You could have a coffin iron bound. And then what good's your contract to me and my brother?" Les said.

Joe only snorted.

"You have a plan for how three guns are going to keep a lid on this town until you hear back?" Seth said.

"The Twisted Tree boys have their hands full gathering those runaways. Especially since they're short-handed." Joe nodded toward the men glowering his way through the bars. "It'll be quiet for now until they work a bulge up again."

"You know you're a dead man," Billy Carruthers said, grinning from the cell door.

"While I'm gone why don't you throw a few buckets of soapy water over those boys? They stink to knock a fly off a shit wagon," Joe said and stepped out onto the boardwalk.

The day was quiet but for a thunderstorm that swept down on Mercury Wells after sundown. The streets turned into a swamp under the driving downpour. The few folks about in the dark kept indoors, crowded into the remaining saloons and cathouses.

Joe donned an oilskin slicker and patrolled the boardwalks alone. As Joe promised, the Twisted Tree crew were absent from town. The drovers off the Three Rivers were somewhere else as well. Homer Gibbs and his cowboys were nowhere in sight. Maybe Hector Nostrand was keeping them back at the bunkhouse. More likely they were still out rounding up strays from the stampede that morning. Or maybe getting their own herd ready for the freight cars coming the next day.

There were a few of the usual fist fights over a woman or hand of cards. Joe let them play out when he found them. Once one drunk was down for the count, he fined both combatants a five dollar cash fine and booted them out into the rain to sober up. One fella pulled a fierce looking knife on a monte dealer. Joe let him off with a dent in his head and a busted arm. There was no room in his cells for more rowdies.

The organ at the Majestic was in competition with rolling crashes of thunder each time the sky was split with streaks of light. The organist was banging out a waltz with a pair of drunks shuffling around the floor in the arms of a pair of indifferent whores. The rest of the patrons either played muted hands of cards or sought the bottom of bottles at the long bar.

Joe stepped to the bar, aware of the eyes on him. He'd long ago learned to discern the difference between idle curiosity and studied intent. Though he was certainly not beloved in this place he didn't sense the frisson of tension that always came before tempers rose to violent action.

He took the offer of a complimentary nip from Marcelle DeGeaux. The sweet fire cut the chill of the wet night. It was top shelf stuff. An aged brandy the Frenchman kept for himself and special visitors.

"Your friend is here," DeGeaux said, nodding toward Ben Temple seated at a table under the stairs. Ben was speaking, telling one of his tales to a glassy-eyed whore with hair the color of brass.

"I saw him," Joe said.

"But did he see you?" Marcelle said with a smirk.

"Trust me, that old badger knows I'm here."

"Has there been a *contretemps* between old friends?"

"He can be a prickly pear. No lie."

"A man needs friends. No man more than you, marshal," DeGeaux said, pouring another dram into Joe's tumbler.

"It's the quality of a man's friends not the number," Joe said.

"The same can be said of a man's enemies."

Joe raised his eyes to lock onto the Frenchman's. Just for a second, DeGeaux flinched under the lawman's icy gaze.

"You trying to tell me something?" Joe said.

"Just making the conversation." DeGeaux shrugged, lips pursed.

"Seems like all day long all I'm hearing is people hinting at the world of trouble I'm in. Walking all around the words without saying them. You have something on your mind?"

"Only that you had best tread lightly, marshal. I say this as someone who likes you." DeGeaux smiled, eyes dancing.

He was startled by the sudden rush of Joe's right hand snaking out to catch a fistful of his silk shirt and pulling him against the bar. The brass trim along the bar struck him hard at the belt line.

"I don't like you, you coon-ass son of a bitch. And I don't like these buttermilk threats I've been getting since I woke up this morning," Joe said between his teeth.

The greasy charm melted from the Frenchman's face. His eyes narrowed and he showed his own teeth between thin lips.

"Only a very foolish man stays where he is not wanted," DeGeaux hissed.

"Then I'll be walking." Joe released the man's shirt front. DeGeaux retreated from his reach. The marshal felt every eye in the house on his back as he made his way to the door and out under the angry sky.

32

Joe Wiley slept past noon the following day. The smell of warm bread and sizzling steak awoke him. He ate breakfast brought over from the Grand Prairie with the Dugans. He took a walk along the boards to stretch his bones and clear the sleep from his head.

A work crew of Chinese was filling the ruts left by last night's storm from a barrow of sand. A crew was raising new tents in place of the ones that burned in the wake of the stampede. The fall of hammers rang out from carpenters nailing the face back on the front of the Dollar Store. The proprietor was out front removing goods from a wagon hitched in the street. He was balancing himself on duck boards under an armload of white fabric he could barely see over.

Joe watched the man, a German named Stroud or Strauss, walk with ginger steps along the planks laid atop the clinging mud of the street. The tubby little man was almost balletic in his attempts to keep his shoes out of the muck. Joe's eyes moved to his burden, a heap of dresses all in white cloth. His eyes turned to slits. He stepped off the boardwalk to intercept the merchant.

The German started at the sudden, painful, grip on his arm. The marshal lifted him to his toes and almost dragged him up onto the boardwalk between two carpenter's ladders. He was shoved against the door jamb of his own store, the pile of dresses hugged to his chest.

Joe took a sleeve of one of the dresses to inspect it. The collar was decorated with embroidery that mimicked the vines of a rose tree. The front was lined with delicate frogs that hooked over cloth covered buttons. Along the sleeve and over one breast was a pink stain. The cloth showed signs of being scrubbed with lye soap in a vain attempt to wash away the stain. He tore the dress from the German's grasp. He riffled the fabric between his fingers. The feel of it was familiar to his touch. He remembered the living warmth of the body that it once sheathed.

"Where'd you get these?" Joe said. His voice was low, the words meant only for the merchant. The menace was clear on his face like a roiling thunderhead lit from within by anvil lightning.

The German's mouth opened and closed like a fish. His eyes darted.

"Don't even think of trying to lie to me, heinie," Joe said.

"A drummer! A man come through this morning!" the man gasped. "Sold me the wagon. *Alles!* The wagon and all inside it!"

Joe shoved the merchant to the boards. The dresses tumbled to the boardwalk and into the marshy street where they sank into a puddle.

Without a word to anyone Joe Wiley fetched his horse from the livery, saddled it himself, and rode away north along the rutted road that led to the hills beyond.

He came upon the wagons at dusk.

They lay skylined against orange clouds, the ribs stripped of canvas. Buzzards, wings spread aloft from the heat still rising off the scrublands, wheeled clockwise, high above in a column. The tongues of the wagons lay angled to the ground. The traces cut. The mule teams run off or led away.

Joe walked to the wagons firing round after round from his Henry as he went, creating eddies and flurries in the buzzards massed on the ground. They flustered into the air on his approach revealing the pale forms lying still in the creosote brush.

It was meant to look like a Comanche attack. But the attempt was a feeble one. The sign in the soft ground all around showed the impressions of steel shod horses. There were boot soles as well. He'd follow those tracks when his work was done here. He knew in his bones what direction they'd turn.

The women, the sisters, lay as they were left. Their naked skin was black with bruises that stood out against their bloodless flesh. Most had been dispatched with a single round to the skull. One or two were painted deep crimson with spills of blood from slit throats.

He found Adeline Tibbets away from the others. She lay on her belly, legs apart. Her long silken hair, matted with dried blood, hid her face from his sight. Rings of dark bruises about her wrists and ankles. Her fingernails were broken and torn, gummy with dried blood. She'd fought as long as she could. In the end it was of no use other than to mark her attackers as Cain was marked.

He lit the wagon alight and worked by the glow of the blaze. He toiled into the night to wrap each of the bodies in a shroud of canvas cut from the wagon bonnets. He buried each in their own grave and made an outline of stones to mark them.

Adeline's grave was deepest and last. He marked it with a wagon tongue set deep in the soil at her head. He secured a cross brace in place to create a rugged cross. Dawn light set the eastern sky afire by the time the last shovel load was in place. The first rays of the sun struck light off the small silver crucifix that was hung from the marker by a chain.

Joe Wiley stood over the humble heap of soil speaking words that he read from the bullet-shot book held in his filthy hands. He dropped to his knees then and remained there as the shadows grew shorter around him. The smoke from the burning wagon rose to smear the yellow sky.

33

With reluctance the teamster pounded a fist on the jailhouse door. A scowling face appeared at the barred port set at eye height.

"State your business," the man at the port growled.

"Fella gave me a message for you. Told me to bring it to the marshal's office." The teamster was a rangy man with a face seared crimson from the sun. He was just into Mercury Wells with a load of fence wire for the Three Rivers.

"What fella?"

"Didn't give me his name. Met him along the road ten or so miles north of here. His clothes were dusty. Tore a page from a book and wrote a few words before handing it off to me."

"What's the message?"

"I was wondering myself seein' as I can't read a word beyond my own name."

The teamster heard bolt after bolt shot free before the iron strapped door squealed opened.

Seth Dugan took the offered piece of paper and unfolded it. The paper was wrapped around a brass marshal's badge. It was a page ripped from a bible with a ragged hole punched through the center. He stepped back into the gloom and slammed the door closed.

"You're welcome all to hell," the teamster said, marching back to his team of four. He smiled as his fingers fondled the double eagle the stranger had given him for the delivery of the note.

"What the hell's it mean?" Les said after his brother had read him the contents of the short note.

"How should I know? It might as well be Latin for all the sense it makes," Seth spat.

"The old man would know," Les said.

Seth made his way to the Majestic while Les remained behind, locked away in the sweatbox of the jailhouse. Ben Temple was not at the Majestic nor at his room at the Grand Prairie. At last, he found the old blind man sitting in a celestial's tent sipping Chinese tea.

Ben Temple nodded when Seth was finished reciting the contents of the note. He made a fist of his hand, his lips pressed together, and brows furrowed.

"That mean damn all to you, Temple?" Seth said.

"Clear as glass. He's said he's riding for Big Bend country," Ben said, a brittle edge to his voice, no trace of his usual glib humor.

"Why in hell? Nothing down there but Mexicans, army deserters, breeds and Christ only knows what manner of two-legged animal." Seth studied the old man's face for sign. Temple's visage turned to a mask of stone.

"You and your brother best split the kitty and ride. Wait till dark and let those men you're holding free. Then get clear of Mercury Wells."

"You gone crazy. My brother and me gave Joe our word we'd stick with him, see the law done here."

"It won't be the law riding with him when Joe comes back." Ben slammed a fist on the table. The cup of tea toppled to send a scalding spill across the wooden top.

"I've known Joe Wiley a long time. And I can't just ride off and leave him. If he's coming back to this shithole, he'll find the Dugans standing where he left us." Seth was losing patience with the old coyote sitting before him talking nonsense.

Ben Temple looked up then, locking eyes on Seth Dugan as if he was seeing the manand seeing him whole. Or more like his blind eyes were seeing *into* the man. His brows relaxed, unraveling. The hard line of his mouth softened. He was seeing past Seth Dugan, seeing something only he had witnessed.

"I've known Joe Wiley longer than you. Almost his whole life. I knew an entire different man than the man you think you understand him to be. I saw him become a man and then make himself, by pure guts and will, into someone else. But that younger fella, that feral wolfling, is still there inside, lying deep. And something's caused that younger Joe to stir again to the surface."

Seth Dugan stood regarding Ben Temple who was sagging at the shoulders now, head drooping. The years were piling up on Ben now all in a moment. The old blind man continued, voice rasping.

"He's coming back here, all right. You can count on that like you can the next sunrise or like you can count on snow in the high ranges come winter. But this time he ain't bringing the law with him. You think yourself a hard man, Dugan. You and your brother both. And by the lights of these days, I suppose you *are* hard men. Only you ain't never seen what these blind eyes have seen and you ain't never seen the Joe Wiley that's going to ride out of Big Bend with all damnation riding behind him."

Ben trailed away to silence and sat unmoving, hand still fisted, eyes peering back across the years.

There were no words left to hear. Seth crushed the bible page in his fist and dropped it in the steaming pool of tea. He backed from the tent and strode to the jailhouse without looking to either side of him.

Billy Carruthers woke late that night with a rumbling in his guts. That damned greasy mess of fried beans and eggs they served them for supper. He clambered over Nestor Ortiz and stumbled to the bucket in the corner. He touched the bucket with the toe of his sock and the contents sloshed over the lip onto the floor soaking his foot. The damn bucket was filled to the brim with piss and shit.

"Hey!" he called; face pressed to the bars. "Shit bucket's full! You gotta toss this out."

No answer from the dark room beyond.

"I'm serious now. My ass is set to blow wide open any second. 'Less you want to mop up after me…"

He expected a retort to that. Especially from the meaner of the pair of brother deputies. Still there was only silence from the gloom. Billy leaned harder into the bars, shifting his cheek against the cold metal for a better angle on the room where the lawmen spent every night playing cards or swapping bullshit.

His weight caused the door to give. He pressed a hand to the bars and pushed. The door swung open, hinges squealing. With one piss-soaked foot in front of the other he crept from the cell toward the marshal's office. Blue moonlight came in through the bars of the narrow port set high on the jailhouse door. Deep shadows described the shape of a table, chairs, standing desk and an empty rack for shotguns and rifles set up against a wall.

And no lawmen, not a one, anywhere to be seen.

34

Bob Miller, county constable, could barely make sense of what he was seeing down at the Majestic. The interior of the saloon looked like a cyclone had blown through. Broken furniture and glass lay about. The face of the fine mirror hanging behind the bar, shipped from St. Louis at great expense, was marred with cracks. A number of men lay insensate on the floor. A drover leaned on the bar hugging a broken arm to his belly. A scene of violence typical of the night life in a cow town and an expected feature in the life of any Texas lawman.

Except for the madly raving blind man standing in the center of the ring of men.

Ben Temple was raging drunk. He held the end of a broken chair leg in one hand and an ugly little derringer in the other. His normally dapper suit of clothes was scruffy and torn. Blood ran down his face to stain his collar from a gash across his brow.

"You have been judged! You have all been judged and found wanting!" the blind man roared, turning this way and that to threaten the men around him. The ring wafted and waned, looking for an opportunity to rush Temple.

"He is a maniac! I want him out of here!" Marcelle DeGeaux was shouting from behind the shelter of the long bar.

Bob waved a calming hand to the Frenchman and shouldered his way through the circle of men.

"Temple, you've had enough for one evening," he said loudly with a firm tone he hoped sounded friendly to the blind man's ears.

"Who's that? Who's talking to me?" Ben said, wheeling to aim the twin barrels of the knucklebuster at the source of the voice.

"It's Bob Miller. County constable. I think you oughta come along with me."

"You've been judged as well, Miller! Mercury Wells has been judged! It teeters at the edge of the fiery pit!" White spittle flew from Temple's lips.

The other constables assigned to the town, five in all, arrived at the doors of the Majestic. Miller held a hand out toward them. They remained in a clutch, ready to assist.

"Ben, you settle down now. Drop that chair leg and that two-shot."

"You will be cast into the outer darkness! There will be a wailing and gnashing of teeth!" Ben still raved but his voice was trailing away now. His arm trembled with the effort of holding the derringer straight.

"You toss those weapons down and come with me, Ben."

"I'm to be taken into custody? Locked away in a cell?" Ben dropped his hands to his sides.

"Only till you sleep it off," Bob Miller said. He stepped forward to pluck the derringer from the blind man's hand. He pulled the chair leg free as well and tossed it to the floor.

"I will go peaceably, Bob. I welcome the solitude, son." Ben surrendered his hands to the constables who rushed in to manacle his wrists together and hustle him out to the street.

35

The line had gone dead. He could feel it in the tips of his fingers.

Red Ferguson had worked as a telegrapher for more than a decade now and had a knowledge of the key earned over thousands of messages sent and received over the singing wires. He'd worked remote mining camps, water stops and tank towns like Mercury Wells. He could tell by the signature rhythm who was on the other end of the line, read the familiar touch of other wire men he knew. He could tell by the cadence who was on the other end of the line, read the accustomed trace of wire men he knew. And he knew when the line he was sending on was dead.

He was in the middle of an inquiry from the local cattleman's association when he felt the key under his fingers go dull. The message was being sent up the line to Barrow where it would be sent on to Abilene in search of the latest per-pound quote for beef on the hoof.

To confirm the break he keyed "stop message" and began a new stream of code requesting a reply from the telegrapher at Barrow. He waited ten minutes and received no answer. Red sent a new message down the line to the rail camp near the ford at Little Deer Creek. No answer.

Red felt a chill grow up his spine to cause his thinning hair to stand on his scalp.

One break in the line could be blamed on wind or some other force of nature. Two breaks, one east and one west of Mercury Wells, could only be the hand of man. There'd been no Comanche raids through the nearby counties since he was a boy in school. Not to say that some of those bastards might not have jumped the reservation to raise a little hell.

He ran from the Texas and New Orleans office into the night-dark street. Red Ferguson was midway to the jailhouse when he heard a rhythmic percussion from somewhere beyond the lights of the town.

The thunder of hooves.

36

It was chaos blowing in out of the night without warning.

The riders struck from every direction at once.

Mexicans on high-cantle saddles. White men on branded-over US army mounts. Breeds riding river-broke paints and dappled grays. Negro vaqueros in tooled chaps and broad sombreros. The kind of men found in the rough country either side of the border. The only unifying feature visible on the riders were the sashes of white cloth tied about their waists under their gun belts.

Riding at their head was a man in black. A rider dressed in a preacher's garb. A long coat with a white sash bound beneath an unusual left-hand rig with a cross-draw holster athwart the buckle.

Whooping and shrieking they raced along the main drag to raise a cloud of dust that wreathed the storefronts in a pale fog. Anyone in the street or on the boardwalks fell in a rain of lead fired wild from the army of mounted men. Some of the riders ducked low in the saddle to ride directly into saloons and tents, opening up with their guns on patrons dazed by drink or sluggish following intercourse. More fell to rounds fired blind through glass and canvas. Men and women fled from a bordello tent only to be crushed under the hooves of the mounted invaders.

The real work of slaughter began when the marauding army dismounted. They invaded every standing structure. The blast of guns competed with the screams of the inhabitants now at the mercy of men who knew no mercy.

It was late in the night when the raid fell upon the town and the Majestic was already shuttered for the night. The pounding of rifle butts on the barred front door was answered by gun fire from within. Raiders fell dead on the boardwalk while others retreated to the street under fire from the second-floor windows. A horse dropped with a bullet through the skull. A pitched battle began as more raiders converged to take cover and lay a fusillade on the building.

Despite round after round peppering the walls of the saloon, the answering rifle and shotgun fire continued from within. A Comanchero tumbled to the street with his spine severed by a big buffalo round. A Mex knelt by a trough and bubbled wordless sounds between the fingers that held what was left of a face ruined by a load of buck.

A wild Texican spurred his roan close enough to the front of the Majestic to send a lit oil lamp through a window on an overhand throw. He was trapped under his kicking mount when the horse fell with a pair of hot rounds through its belly. A rifle round took off the top of his skull as he fought to free his trapped leg from beneath the panicked animal.

The thrown lamp found a home within, shattering along a carpeted floor. The hungry flames spread up the papered walls to find dry wood beams and framework. The second floor was an inferno inside of seconds. Thick black smoke bled from every window and seam. Guttural screams of men resonated from inside along with the piercing keen of whores trapped in the blazing building. Men clambered out onto the roof of the porch to be pitched backwards by concentrated rifle and pistol fire from the street below. The screams of the women died away as the embers rose into the night sky.

Marcelle DeGeaux himself exploded from a back door, his clothes smoldering from the furnace heat he'd escaped. He fired blind into the surrounding shadows only to be brought down by men laughing as they took aim. They pumped rounds into his trembling body as they stepped closer in a half circle. He was still in his dying throes as they began stripping him of valuables. A half-Wichita breed grew frustrated with the Frenchman's struggles and took to biting the ring fingers from each palsied hand.

The on-duty constables spilled from the jailhouse only to fall to a storm of bullets. One of them survived the barrage to stumble back inside and bar the door. He dropped to the floor holding his hand pressed to a rent made in the flesh of his gut. The lawman could feel his failing pulse through the hand he held to a slippery section of bowel trying to spill from the tear. His hand fell away as his strength ebbed, releasing a greasy cascade of innards to the dirty floor. The constable died there, his only witness the solitary prisoner locked away in one of the cells. It was a drunken blind man who saw him to the next world.

Eyes watering from smoke, Billy Carruthers slashed through the canvas with a buck knife to make a new exit at the rear of a tented whorehouse. He exited with an arm about the throat of a mulatto whore and a long-barreled Colt in his hand. He was jay naked except for his boots but more concerned with flight than modesty. He was halfway to the cover of a copse of dogwoods when a pair of riders caught up with him. The Twisted Tree cowboy spun, raising the Buntline too late. A .44-40 punched through the chest of the girl to rip sideways deep into Billy's ribcage. The cowboy fell with the whore atop him and squirmed in a fight to regain his feet. The riders reined in to ride about him in a circle, laughing as they took turns putting rounds through the skinny whore and thus into Billy Carruthers. Both lay still under a gray haze of gun smoke. The riders whooped and spurred away to fresher butchery.

Other cowboys, from the Twisted Tree, Three Rivers and smaller outfits, died all over town either where they lay drunk or in vain efforts to make it to their horses. They died in the dust of the street and atop the stained sheets on the cots of fallen women. They died standing on their feet defiant. They died on their knees pleading for mercy from man and Jesus.

Bob Miller, the acting chief constable of Mercury Wells, crept down the stairs from his room at the Grand Prairie. He was in stocking feet and britches, his boots under one arm and a big Harrington Richardson revolver in his trembling fist. He made it to the foot of the stairs and turned toward the registrar's counter. His immediate design was to make it through the door to the rear of the hotel and from there out into the night where he would find a place to hide until the raiders had spent their wrath on the town.

After all, he was no real lawman. His position was more political in nature. The citizens understood that. It was important that he preserve himself in order to provide leadership in the aftermath of this debacle.

Miller wheeled at a crash of glass. The front doors of the hotel banged open. The high glow of flames at his back, a figure in black strode in to fire a pistol from either hand. Bob Miller stumbled back against the marble-topped registrar desk with twin burning sensations in his chest and belly. The revolver dropped from his nerveless hand.

Joe Wiley stepped across the carpet; pistols trained on the gasping constable. With the toe of a boot, he turned Bob Miller's face to the light. In the wavering glare he could see four parallel furrows in the face of the fallen man, ragged scars still raised even after two weeks of healing.

The pain was closing like a fist deep inside Bob Miller's gut. His breathing was coming hard as one lung filled with blood. Despite the pain, growing in intensity by the second, Bob knew he'd be hours dying.

Joe Wiley's shadow fell over him. He closed his eyes against the killing round but opened them again at the sound of boots stepping away across the floor. He watched the former town marshal stride from the hotel into the flame dappled night, the doors swinging shut behind.

The burning fist inside him closed taut with a renewed fury.

37

It was near to a full week before the Rangers arrived in Mercury Wells. The company of Rangers numbered six men. It was a sign of the pressure placed upon the governor in Austin that so many of the state's lawmen were assigned to site of the massacre.

They found the town much as it was the day following the night of the raid. The only structures that remained standing were the town's three-story hotel and the jailhouse. The rest—stores, saloons, homes and train station—were only described by the blackened skeletal remains of their frames. All that was left of the many tents were broad areas of scorched ground.

Bodies still swung from ropes looped over the arms of telegraph poles. Vultures sat atop the cross braces until dispersed by rifle shots. The lynching victims were lowered to the ground with as much respect as could be had given that each man was either naked or in shit-stained britches.

The hanged men were identified by Hector Nostrand, boss man off a local ranch. He mostly claimed to recognize them by body shape since the buzzards had consumed the softer flesh of their faces. The town mayor, town banker and a railroad man who often had business in Mercury Wells were his best guess as the identities of the hanged. None of that three made any kind of appearance in the week that followed the destruction of Mercury Wells. There were a dozen or more men strung up along the telegraph lines leading to the west. These were assumed to be storeowners or other types of businessmen once prominent in the town.

The death toll was near fifty in town not counting Chinese and whores. All of the town's acting law enforcement, six county constables in total, and an assortment of cowboys, pimps, private police employed by the saloons and others had been executed by the still-unknown raiders. More than a hundred had been spared including the manager of the Grand Prairie, the organist at the Majestic and a prisoner, a blind man, held in the town jail.

The station house had been set ablaze and along with it a half mile section of track. The ties were soaked in lamp oil and touched off. The heat consumed the ties and caused the rails to twist like licorice sticks. A long train of waiting cattle cars were destroyed as well in the fire.

Aside from wholesale murder, arson and vandalism, the raiders also made off with three thousand head of longhorns awaiting transport in the stockyards. No account of how many horses were driven away. The vault that once rested inside the bank had been hauled off as well. Every corpse had been stripped of all valuables even to the amputation of fingers and ears to facilitate the removal of jewelry.

The most reliable witness to these horrors was a young half-breed boy who claimed to have seen "the whole thing" from a hiding place on the other side of the tracks. According to his claim, the raiders numbered in the thousands and were dressed as savages in war paint and feathers. The leader was a Mescalero or Comanche seven feet tall with a wolf's head worn on his head and riding a horse black as a starless night.

The Rangers gave little credence to the boy's story and even less to the testimony of the hotel manager and organist who swore to have seen nothing on the night of raid. There were no other witnesses worth a damn since most of the survivors had departed along the rail line to Barrow and destinations unknown.

The only worthwhile evidence that remained was the broad trail left by three thousand head of cattle still plain as ink on paper even after a week's time. The Rangers followed the trail south until the sign split into two then four then six parties and more going off in as many different directions over the broken ground north of Big Bend country. To separate and chase after such small bands into the arroyos, washes, canyons and passes of the Chisos was folly even for as hardass a bunch as the Texas Rangers. Those beeves were in Mexico by now, far from the reach of any Lone Star authority. And the nameless men along with them.

All that was left was work for the railroad navvies. They would come to bury the dead and patch over the break in the rails. Along with its citizens, Mercury Wells had died as well. The ranches that could recover from their losses would have to drive the herds another hundred miles north. All that would remain of a once thriving town would be a water stop once the tank was rebuilt.

38

The blaze within the stone open hearth washed the well-appointed office with a fiery glow and welcoming heat.

Lined with wooden bookshelves graoning with leather-bound tomes, the center of the room was dominated by a massive mahogany desk. The desktop was ordered and uncluttered. A blotter, a pen and inkwell on one side and a humidor on the other.

At the middle of the desk sat a crystalline chess set of finely etched pieces. A servant stood to one side of the desk with a silver tray waiting for his master's will. On the other stood the massive Sikh bodyguard. Seated behind the desk in a high-backed chair of antelope hide was the limping man, who was reading the note brought to him by the servant. As he read the message the man's brow creased and his face darkened.

The silence of the room was broken when the limping man leaped to his uneven feet and slashed at the chess set with his exquisitely crafted wooden cane, shattering the crystal pieces and sending them asunder in a spray of shards and powder. The servant trembled at the old man's fury. The Sikh stood still and silent as an ancient pillar. Crumpling the note in his hands, the limping man looked up at his huge bodyguard.

"Find this man Joe Wiley. Wherever he is under the sun. And provide him with an agonizing death," the old man said as cold as winter.

The Sikh touched the hilt of his dagger and bowed before, wordlessly, turning to leave the presence of his employer.

39

The tiny, lazy cantina provided one of the few places free from the sweltering afternoon sun that baked the land ruled by Juarez.

Outside of the squat adobe building the streets were empty aside from a handful of locals having their siesta in any available shade. Inside the cantina was a simple but welcoming environment, the air cooler and stirred by a boy working a hand fan with a foot pedal for ten American cents a day. Bottles of sangria, tequila, and whiskey were lined up behind the bar. A large Mexican man sat behind the bar, his brushy mustache covering a third of his fat face. He slumbered, leaning on the bartop. He absent-mindedly swatted at a fly, murdering it with surprising speed before returning to his afternoon nap. His only customers were two gringos seated in the dimmest corner of the great room, both in chairs that faced the bar of sunlight at the cantina's only entrance.

Seated at the corner table were Joe Wiley and Ben Temple. A bottle of whiskey, two shot glasses and a deck of cards between them.

"Your deal," Joe said.

He watched as the old man effortlessly shuffled the deck despite his blindness.

"I'll never get over how you do that. Or how you seem to always win." Joe shook his head.

"Practice son. Practice and faith in the Lord," Ben answered him.

Joe let out a snort at that.

As the blind old man dealt the hand Joe looked out from the shadows of the cantina and into the brutal heat. He looked past the humble little shacks to the flat landscape with mountains of faded blue limning the horizon. And his mind wandered for a moment back to Mercury Wells and Sister Adeline Tibbets. He shook off the haunting memory and gathered his hand.

Two deuces. An eight of spades. A queen of heart and a four of clubs.

"Damn you, old man," he said. But Ben could hear the reluctant smile in his voice. He kept the smile from his own face as he examined a full house, ace high.

"Too late for that, son. Far too late for that."

END

About the Authors

CHUCK DIXON is the prolific author of thousands of comic book scripts for *Batman and Robin, the Punisher, Nightwing, Conan the Barbarian, Airboy, the Simpsons, Alien Legion* and countless other titles.

Together with Graham Nolan, Chuck created the now iconic Batman villain Bane. He also wrote the international bestselling graphic novel adaptation of J.R.R. Tolkien's *The Hobbit.*

He currently writes two series for Bruno Books: the time travel epic Bad Times, as well as the ebook sensation Levon Cade. He also adapted Peter Schweitzer's controversial bestseller *Clinton Cash* into a graphic novel.

Visit his website at chuckdixon.net or enjoy his YouTube channel, *Ask Chuck Dixon.*

He calls Florida home these days.

Visit the Dixonverse!

Little is known about the stranger named JOHN MORGAN NEAL. He lives (*Clap Clap Clap Clap*) deep in the heart of Texas in a four color coma. He writes some comics and has read a LOT of comics books. He also likes to watch and make movies. He co-created the comic characters Aym Geronimo and the PostModern Pioneers© with artist Todd Fox. He is Captain Moderator Jr. at the Dixonverse©. He was a founder, partner, editor and writer at the long lost Shooting Star Comics. He was the co-creator of *Gone to Texas* and *Rex Solomon* along with Gregg Noon, and the soon to debut *THEM: Atomic Age Heroes!* along with artist and co-creator Rob Bavington. He has a puppy dog named Bones© who watches TV with him. He now resides (in his Batman© jammies and Thing© feet slippers) at the Arkham Asylum© for the Terminally Bewildered and looks forward to Fish sticks and Jell-O© night. Some say he may be the Psychotronic Man.

Visit John Neal's website www.aymgeronimo.com .

www.ingramcontent.com/pod-product-compliance
Ingram Content Group UK Ltd.
Pitfield, Milton Keynes, MK11 3LW, UK
UKHW041847190726
13854UKWH00002B/757